FEDERATED INTERSTELLAR TACTICAL SQUAD

F.I.S.T.S

HANDBOOK FOR INDIVIDUAL SURVIVAL IN HOSTILE ENVIRONMENTS

By Bey Deckard

Property of:

ABOUT THE TYPE
Natanael Gama - SIL Open Font License, 1.1
Exo is a contemporary geometric sans serif typeface that tries to convey a technological/futuristic feeling while keeping an elegant design. Exo was meant to be a very versatile font, so it has 9 weights (the maximum on the web) each with a true italic version. It works great as a display face but it also works good for small to intermediate size texts.

CONTENTS

1. Sarge
2. Murphy
3. The Missing Reel

SARGE

BEY DECKARD

For JLT

MURPHY

Down on my knees in mud made from equal parts dirt and blood, I survey the damage done to Sarge. His left eye's completely gone; it's just a big, wet red hole where the charge went in. Thankfully, it's cauterized some, so the bleeding is minimal. There's nothing I can really do about it; he'll have to get it replaced at the chop 'n' change at HQ, and that's a half-hour hike that might as well be on the other side of the planet as long as the sun's still up.

I pop open a compartment in my hip and take out a pin-sticker of hubba bubba. I jab it into his neck and sit back to check if any of this goddamned blood is my own while I let the painkiller work its magic. HeBA, or Hexa-Benactryl Almeanotroxene, is a synthetic compound that's part homegrown and part alien; the fact that the shit is bright fucking pink gets me thinking that the squinters and grinders that make it were actively hoping for the nickname.

It doesn't take long. The hubba's pretty potent. Up until this point, he's been staring off to the side, his face tense, not saying a word. The wound's gotta hurt like hell, but this is *Sarge*. He's a legend. Hell, even I'd be tempted to cry a little if some asshole blew a hole in my head. When he finally turns to me, his right eye looks blankly somewhere over my shoulder, and there's no expression on his face.

"Marine?" he says, like he doesn't know who I am. He's still not looking directly at me, and it dawns on me right then that maybe he can't see.

"Y'sir," I reply. My voice is in the basement end of the register, all gravel and boom. Half of what I say ends up sounding like a grunt, but that's fine with me. I don't say much.

"I think I'm blind," he says, blinking slowly. It seems like his marbles are all in place though; he doesn't have that lost look that most men got in his situation. I nod, and then feel like an idiot.

"Y'sir," I say again. I reach for his face. "Uh, hang on. Sorry." To his credit, he doesn't look alarmed when I start stuffing the empty socket with gauze before taping the whole thing over with a few strips of med tape. When I'm done sealing the damage, I thumb up the lid from the other eye. The pupil's not reacting to the light from my helmet, so I figure there's something wrong between his eye and his brain.

I get a bright idea and dig around in the med-kit some more. I find the relays and press one to his right temple before sticking one to my own. They both come on, powered by the subtle electric charge that runs through a human body. I watch the little LEDs go through their patterns as they calibrate, but I have no fucking clue if this is going to work. These relays are made for bridging the neural gap caused by injury in one individual—you know, so that a guy with a spinal injury can still hoof it to HQ on his own. I don't know if lending a little of my brain's processing power to his eye is going to result in anything good. Maybe I'll just end up short-circuiting my own damn head, but it's worth a try.

I'd give my fucking life for this man.

After a few seconds, Sarge blinks, looking startled. His pupil contracts when he turns and focuses on me. I don't feel any worse for wear, so I figure the relays are doing their job. They're good for about two metres and change, so he and I are going to have to stick close, but that really doesn't bother me.

"Murphy?" he says, surprised. "How in the hell did you know that was going to work?" He looks at the relay on my face and touches the one on his own.

"Didn't," I reply. It comes out as a mumble, but he doesn't notice because he's suddenly peering around in confusion.

Oh shit.

"What the hell? What are all these colours? Is this a side

effect?" he asks. There's a loud boom to the north of us, and I see the streak of blue across my vision. I watch his eye track it.

"Erm, no Sarge," I say. "Synesthesia." It feels like a lie. What I have is not the run-of-the-mill, smells-or-sounds-to-colours kinda thing. Somehow, I'm able to pick up on waves in the air, and my brain neatly colour-codes them for me. You know the electricity I mentioned before that runs through every one of us? Well, that gives off waves too, and it changes with emotions. Not exactly something I like to advertise; I'm already a bit of a freak. I wonder with a grimace what Sarge will make of what he sees.

Needing something to do with my hands, I take the rifle from his lap and begin to strip it down.

"It's... beautiful," he says, gesturing to the air in front of him.

I grunt a reply and nod, concentrating on the BFG on my knees. The pieces slide into my hands as I hit all the small catches. Though this one is identical to my own, my fingers know it's a stranger. A ding here, a scratch there—every piece unique.

"I take it we're waiting until sundown before heading back to HQ?" he asks, peering at the heat-distorted horizon.

Another nod from me. The sight on his gun's a little sticky so I give it a rub with the cloth from my hip and screw it back into place.

"You ain't much of a conversationalist are you?" asks Sarge after watching me work for a while.

"N'sir," I reply. How can I tell him that every time I open my mouth, I feel like an idiot? I'm not though. It's just that I don't have a way with words like a lot of the other guys do. I'm not funny. I can't tell a story to save my life. I'm not even especially crass, something that would at least make what I said colourful. Nah, I just leave the talking up to other people. That's fine with me.

I finish up with his gun and hand it back to him before starting on my own.

I can tell that he's watching me closely, and it's making me a little uncomfortable. Not really in a bad way, mind you.

"You're a fucking mystery, Murph," he says to me. "I see you eating by yourself, head down, reading something on your pad.

Always on the fringes when we're offstage. No one talks to you. But, when the curtain rises, you've got everyone's back, and you fight like goddamn Mars himself."

I lift my eyes for a sec before looking back down at the rifle I'm turning over in my hands. This is the most Sarge has ever said to me. I just hope my brain's not showing him too much about how thrilled I am; I'm probably lit up like a Christmas tree, and I'm sure that beneath the blood and paint on my face, I'm blushing like a schoolgirl. What would he think about the fact that being around him makes my britches a little tight?

"So you like pain, do you?" he asks, seemingly out of the blue. For a sickening moment, I think he's been following my line of thought. Just as he said it, I was thinking that if Sarge asked me to lick the sole of his boot, I'd have a granite staff in my shorts. But, when I look up, I see that he's staring at my arms.

Now, regulation armour has us covered from chin to ankle in flexible nano-shielding that even a buzz bullet from a GR-U can't cut into. Problem is, unless you're running your cooling unit all the damn time, in a day you'll lose half your body weight in sweat. After five years in this hell of a war with CUs breaking down only weeks into combat, you see a lot of us grunts using the mech torches to cut loose the moulded carapace pads as soon as we get them. Basically, I look like I'm wearing glorified football shoulder pads with elbow, knee, and ass pads to match.

The whole thing used to be painted a dark blue, the colour of my unit, but since then I've taken a half-hundred hits, and the paint's mostly chipped off. It's a dull, dark grey with hints of gore at the moment. There's webbing down the front of my chest where there's a series of compartments to keep my stuff—you'd be amazed how much you can carry when you strip out the plate lining them—but, apart from the shorts and the helmet I mentioned earlier, I've got nothing else on. I don't care; I'd rather get shot than die from dehydration.

The reason Sarge is staring at my arms is because of the colourful tattoos that cover me from shoulder to knuckle; you can see them clear as day between the straps that hold the moulded pads of my armour in place. They're a combination of *Irezumi* and laser etching—something the kids these days call "slash and burn"—and are taken from the margins of an illustrated book of poetry my mum used to read to me as a kid. They're what you'd call "fanciful" if you were the type to use that kind of word. Songbirds, dragons, butterflies, insects; it's like my skin is the sky, and it's filled with colourful things in flight. I feel silly just thinking that, but hell, I like the way they look.

Sarge hasn't said anything to merit a gruff *thanks* from me; I can't tell if he actually likes them or if he's just going to leave it at the question about pain. I'm about to shrug my shoulders and go back to putting the BFG back together when he looks into my eyes.

He's curious. He's also impressed.

There's a little dry spot at the back of my throat, so I swallow hard and end up coughing into my fist. I realize then that maybe the question wasn't rhetorical like I figured; what if he wanted an honest-to-goodness answer from me? On a crazy impulse, I decide to give him one.

"Y'sir," I manage to mumble, my voice in the basement again. I look down and realize I'm thumbing the tit of the power switch like I'm trying to get it hard, and my cheeks get hot again.

To distract myself, I pick up the little collapsible pot from the lip of the trench and gently slide the circle of nano-plastic from the top of it. After I fold away the water-harvester into quarters to stow away, I feel a little reckless and take out a metal thimble. Sarge watches me quietly as I float it in the piss-warm water that collected in the pot. I slap the side of my rifle to release the coolant pod and, with a practiced hand, I pop open the side and let a single drop fall into the thimble. Instantly, ice crackles over the surface of the water, and I lift the thimble out. I look up, slightly shamefaced for showing off now, and offer the water to Sarge.

He accepts it with a wry grin.

Using coolant from a CP to make water cold is illegal for two reasons: one, the stuff is completely poisonous; so much as a drop gets into a gallon of water, and you'll be shitting your brains out and sweating like a pig for hours. Second, taking coolant out of your weapon is considered a criminal waste of resources. That one makes no fucking sense anymore; I'm literally sitting in a trench full of dead guys, and every single one of them has a rifle with a CP in it. It's not like I'm going to hump them all back to HQ with me. Sarge, of course, knows all this, and I can't believe I just had the stones to flaunt it in his fucking face. He takes a sip and hands it back to me. However, I don't see anything but amusement from him; my stupid party trick's not going to land me in the stockade this time. I breathe easier, though I feel little sheepish.

"What were you doing before the war, son?" he asks, leaning back against the wall of the dig-in; he knows we've got at least another hour to wait before the massive red sun dips below the horizon, so he's making conversation.

For a second, I'm a little disappointed. If he'd taken a look at my sheet, he would've known that about me; I'm embarrassed by the number of times I've looked at his. I take a deep breath and stare down at my boots. I'm ankle deep in slime and, for a split second, I'm struck by how so sick and tired of the fucking war I am.

It passes.

"Studyin', Sarge," I reply after a thought.

"In what?"

"Neuroscience." The word barely makes it out of my mouth before I quickly take another sip of water and roll it over my tongue. The startled silence is one that I'm really fucking familiar with.

Sarge sees my discomfort; maybe it's the relay showing him, or maybe he's just observant, but he lets out a small laugh. He takes the pot out of my hand, and his fingers graze mine. I feel a little weird. Maybe the relay's doing something to my brain after all. Maybe it's just my fucking nerves.

"Murph, you gotta admit that you don't seem the type," he chides me.

See, I'm a big guy. I'm just about 6'8 in my boots. A slab of muscle on a frame that's almost comically large. Pair that with the fact that I don't say much, and you've got people thinking I'm none too bright. The big dumdum that can tear the arm off an enemy soldier if he's in the right mood. I shrug. I'm good at shrugging.

"So, you're smart. I'm not that surprised actually, given your idea with the neuro-relays. Got a girl back home, Murphy? A wife?" he asks. When I shake my head no, he gives another little laugh. A pause. "A man, then?" Another shake of my head, but this time my face is so hot you could cook a fucking egg on it. "What? Single? A good-looking guy like you? I find that hard to believe, son."

The way he calls me *son* does something to me. Everyone always thinks that because I look like a big, mean bastard, I'm the dominant type. I can't count the number of times that I've disappointed guys.

When I look up again, I see that his one eye is narrowed at me in amusement. And something... else. Without an ounce of diffidence, he casually asks me another question.

"So, are you completely proportionate?"

It takes me a second, maybe two, before I realize that he's asking whether I'm packing a peashooter or a rocket launcher in my shorts. We're out hiding from enemy soldiers, buried ankle deep in the guts of our unit and burning under an alien sun, him missing an eye, and he's asking about my fucking cock. Sarge is *hitting on me*. There's no mistaking the gleam in his eye, and I can see it coming off of him in waves.

You could not have painted me more shocked.

He gives this little laugh and adds, "Well?" when I don't reply right away.

I turn away to stare at the horizon, a huge shit-eating grin on my face that won't budge. After a sec, I just give a little nod. I know I'll be crushed if he wants to call me "Daddy" or some shit, but at least for now, I couldn't be happier. However, a second later he removes any of my doubts.

"You're a good boy, Murph," he says softly to me. "You get

me home, get me patched up, and you'll see what good boys get."

I swear to god, I have never made a sound like it before; half whimper, half gasp, it's past my lips before I can stop it. Sarge sees the effect his words have on me, and he smiles. It takes me a few loud beats of my heart to realize he's waiting for me to answer. I let my own grin drop, digging around in my skull for my usual serious sense of duty. I give a nod, swivelling the scope from my rifle between my fingers.

"Aye'sir," I rumble, and his grin widens.

With a new sense of purpose, I turn to the horizon and drop the sun shielding over the charge rifle's sight so I won't blind myself. I squint and peer. The coast is clear, as far as I can tell. Maybe we don't need to wait until after sunset after all.

Without glancing back, I know that Sarge is thinking the same thing.

SARGE

With what I figure's my tenth sigh in as many minutes, I throw the pad down on the desk and give it my best fuck-you-call-me-*Sir*-goddamn-it look. Works on the men, but this is just a fucking pad, and it sits there beeping its annoying little beep as it waits for me to finish my goddamn rec 'n' ditch list.

See, I'm on the mend. I'm supposed to be *taking it easy* while all the nerves and what-have-yous heal up properly. They don't want me to fuck up the replacement job they did on me, and shit, that's fine. I get it. But taking it easy's for old men, and I'm not quite ready to admit to that yet.

I run my fingertips around my eye socket, right along the edges of the implant where the skin still feels a little numb to the touch, and can't hold back another goddamned sigh. I know it'll feel just like my own worn hide in a couple of weeks—after all, this ain't my first rodeo, as they used to say—but I can't help but be a lick impatient.

I shouldn't be complaining. Hell... in my day? Back in my day, you didn't get a new eyeball if some shit-sucking alien cowboy blew it out with a charge rifle. No, back in my day, you had to suffer your goddamn injury and keep your yap shut until you got shipped off to one of the bigger colonies. These days, you get serviced almost on-the-spot by kids who barely passed their Med-Ones before they were given a license to slice, dice, 'n' splice. Everything is so fucking automated now. Shit, how long is it before there's no room left in this goddamn war for real warriors? It'll be machine versus machine soon enough...

I laugh at myself and rub my face some more, trying to steer my thoughts away from being put out to pasture with nothing but a golden handshake and a whole lotta fruit salad pinned to my chest. My chair lets out an oil-thirsty whine when I swivel it to take in the view of something that always gets my mind off my damn troubles.

Murphy's on his knees, facing away from me. I've got him spit-shining boots that don't really need to be spit-shined, but he does such a goddamn pretty job of it that I have him do it every chance I get. I sit back in my chair and cross my arms, admiring the display. The boy's in nothing but his regulation knee pads and boots, and I feel a mild surge in my shorts at the sight of the thick piece of meat that swings between his muscled thighs as he leans forward to grab something. He's gorgeous, this kid; big as a goddamned wall and built like a Roman god.

I cluck my tongue once to get his attention, and he turns right away. I fucking love how attentive he is. Still on his knees with thighs spread, he puts his ankles together and his hands behind his back, keeping his chin down as he waits... just like the good boy he is. But, right now, I really want to see those eyes, and Murphy knows better than to look up without being asked.

"Son," I say real low, but it's enough for him to raise his head. He's got a good-looking face: a square jaw, a nose that looks like it's only been broken maybe once, nice-shaped eyebrows that are a bit darker than the short fuzz of mouse-brown hair on his skull, full lips that pucker in at the corners, the bottom one dimpled by a thin scar that curves down and over his chin. But it's really the sum of the parts that makes him so damned handsome, something he obviously doesn't believe about himself, given the way his forehead wrinkles every time I pay him a compliment.

His best feature, however, is those goddamn eyes.

When he lifts them to look at me, I feel the soft rush I always do when confronted with that wide, crystal-blue gaze. The closest feeling I can bring to mind is that first morning I saw Terra's blue waters from outside the old space hulk's pitted windows... Those vast oceans still hiding ancient secrets though humankind had taken to the sky generations before. It just triggers something in me, like a memory buried deep. I realise it's a weird fucking thought, and for the umpteenth time I wonder if what I'm feeling is a side effect of the neuro-link we shared through those cheap, med-kit relays.

"Are you nearly done with my boots?" I ask just to have something to say. Murphy nods only once, never one to waste actions. His skin shines damp in the dim yellow light of my quarters—we never escape this wretched fucking heat—and I watch a trickle of sweat slide over his collarbone to follow the thick, twisted scar that runs from his left pec to the hip bone opposite. A couple years back, Murphy got caught in a reaver's cave, and he was damn near killed.

I'm glad he wasn't.

As always, his expression is a combination of admiration, shyness, and relief. It's that last one that always gets me. The boy was so quick to give me the reins that it makes me wonder for a moment what the hell happened to him to make him this way. That, of course, always leads me to wonder about my own fucked-up appetites, and, really, that's something I'd rather not delve into... Who the shit cares, right? I'm just glad I only had to pay an eye for what I tend to look upon as a goddamn prize won.

I don't even have to say anything; I just shift my legs a bit wider and place my hands on the worn arms of the chair. Murphy lifts himself up right away and buries his face in my blues, those nice lips of his honing in on the head of my cock through two layers of fabric and squeezing it with a little huff of hot breath. He nibbles at it through my pants a little more but not too much. He won't tease. No, he's smarter than that. Knows that while I won't be kept waiting, a little warm-up is always welcome.

By the time he unzips my fly and reaches into my shorts to grab my dick, I'm filling up his big hand with every passing heartbeat. It feels fucking great, but the best part is when he opens his mouth a second later and says the thing that always near kills me:

"Can I, Sarge?"

Like my cock is a goddamned golden staff that he needs permission to put his lips around. I love it.

With my nod, he goes straight to it.

I watch him lick carefully at the plump crown, his warm, wet tongue sliding softly, leaving cool streaks over skin that's getting more and more taut and shiny. He sucks in the head so slowly, like he's savouring every moment, tongue stroking me in a lazy circle, that when I feel the edges of my cockhead breach the tight hold of his lips, I let out a long, low groan and shift my hips eagerly. The kid's good at what he does.

I reach down to touch his brush cut and then let my thumb slide down the side of his jaw—just to let him know I'm pleased— and he looks up at me, mouth full of my cock and big blue eyes wide. I can't help but think to myself that, shit, this is the goddamned life.

Murphy pulls back a little, and my cock pops out from between his lips, spit-wet and throbbing with my pulse. I'm about to object when he turns his head and takes my thumb into his mouth instead. He gnaws at it all gentle, teeth and tongue teasing over my fingerprint, before he slides it further so that my hand winds up cupping his jaw. His mouth is hot and wet and when he sucks softly, I get an unexpected, almost electric pulse that shoots straight to my groin; it's damned sexy what he's doing. Sexy and something else. It only lasts a few seconds before he's back to sucking me off with a skill that has me straining back in my chair, my eyes closed as I groan my encouragement.

"That's it. A little faster. You love having my big cock in your mouth, don't you, son? Oh. Oh... That's a good boy..."

He's working it down his throat like a pro until he jerks slightly with a little, convulsive cough meaning he's finally hit his limit; but, like the eager kid he is, he pulls back only briefly before gorging himself on my cock again. It's like he's fucking starving for it.

I wrap both hands around his throat. With my splayed fingers underneath and my thumbs at his nape—Murphy's neck so big that my fingers don't meet—I feel the way my cock shoves his tongue down into the soft tissues beneath his jaw, pressing against my fingers as I fuck his throat. Again I feel that spasm as he gags, and I think I'm about to blow my load, but instead I push him back.

Panting with lips wet and shiny, Murph looks at me in a daze, but he's quick to put his hands behind his back again just like I taught him. I think I can see a little disappointment in his face. Murphy really gets off on giving head; you can tell by the way his rock-hard cock is bobbing and drooling long strings onto the concrete floor.

Shaft in fist, I start jerking off and tell him to open his mouth. He looks so damned eager as he opens wide, his eyes fixed on my cock, that it takes only a few seconds before the first jet of cum hits his bottom lip. My aim's off, but that's part of what makes this so goddamn hot. I get about half my load on his face, and the rest on his chest and stomach before my balls are hollow and my cock stops throbbing in my hand.

With a happy groan, I just let myself fall back in my chair and close my eyes for a second, just catching my breath. When I open them again, I smile at Murphy, kneeling there with my cum dripping off his chin. He hasn't moved a muscle, and he won't unless I tell him to.

"Tidy up. Start with this," I say and point to my lap with a smile.

"Aye'sir."

The big brute gives another one of his efficient little nods before he leans forward and washes my cock with his tongue, all gentle-like. When he's done, I shove it back in my pants and stand.

I've got a meeting, and I'm never late to these things.

I think for a second about telling Murphy to take care of that raging erection he's got sprouting like a veiny, purple staff between his legs, but he'll keep. He's a good boy, my Murphy; never a peep of complaint when I make him wait for his reward... and reward him I do. I'm a man of my word. Hell, the kid had to carry me up on his fucking back for the last mile across scorched desert. I'll keep rewarding him for as long as he'll stay with an old bastard like me.

I watch him wipe a hand up his chest and then lick his palm clean, his eyes patient and calm like a week of Sundays as he looks up at me from his position on the floor.

I know I'm fucking lucky.

I touch his head briefly before I reach for my pad and head for the War Room.

Fucking goddamn lucky.

MURPHY

I'm contemplating the ceiling that's lost high above me in the dark while stretched out on the floor with just a wadded-up pillow under my head. I really don't need more than that, to be honest. I've been sleeping out in the open for years. Shit, the fact that there's a roof over my head is a luxury.

I'm naked because Sarge likes me that way. And that's fine with me too. After all, my cock is his; if he wants it out in the open, so be it.

Problem is, said cock isn't behaving right now.

So, I'm lying here, stiff as a fence post, unable to sleep and just waiting for morning to come in about thirty minutes. I hear Sarge shift a little up on his cot, and I idly wonder what he dreams about. The thought makes me smile. He'd probably think I was ridiculous for wondering, but hey, I spend almost every moment I can with this man. I want to know everything about him. Not only because I'm curious, but because it might help me to serve him better.

I'm still blown away that he went through the actual proper channels to have me as his bunkmate. Shit, I would have been happy just to stay over, in whatever capacity he wanted me in, but seeing my name on the door below his... I can't even put it to words. Happy doesn't cut it. Proud, maybe. When he ordered me to move my kit to his quarters, I must have looked like a fucking imbecile with my mouth dropped open like I was in one of those old cartoon shows.

I shift a little on the cold concrete. It feels good against my skin, seeing that it's hot as hell in here on account of the sun being at its apex; the cheap shielding of the compound isn't holding up well at these temperatures, and the shitty A/C's on the fritz again. But, for me, it ain't so bad really. Better than that tiny ice chunk those fucking bastards were holed up in last time we came after them. Froze my balls off the whole time.

With that thought, I reach down and scratch my sack lightly, careful not to brush my cock. Sarge told me I wasn't to touch it, and I'm minding him.

Yeah, I'll admit, I'm feeling a little bit tender. It's been days since I've gotten any kind of relief. Not that I've fucked up or anything... He just hasn't given me permission. And, honestly? Despite the fact that I've never been so ridiculously sensitive in my life—fuck, trust me, I'd love to just jack off right now—I've never felt more at peace with myself. He's in control, and he is *pleased* with me. Really pleased.

I just wish my cock would stop throbbing, so I could go back to sleep.

I pass a bunch of guys in the hallway and somehow manage to trip on someone's foot. Then I land in a heap on the floor, scraping my elbows and shit, and I'm turning around to get back up again when I realize that the grunts are all laughing at me for some reason. I look down and see that I'm butt naked, and I've got this really crazy hard-on. Part of me knows that this is fucking weird, but I'm shoving my hands in front of my crotch to hide my boner anyway even though I shower with these same guys every day.

So, this guy I can't remember seeing before walks up and tells the others to get lost. There's a little scuffle and back talk, but they leave, and then he holds out his hand. I've got to let go of my pecker to grab his hand, and fuck, I somehow wind up against the wall with him rubbing himself hard against me.

Again, my brain's telling me that something's fishy, but god he feels good, and when he starts biting my neck and I'm warm and slippery, caught between his bare legs, I feel that sweet little burst deep inside me that spreads out to my balls and through my cock... And next thing I know I'm cumming all over his thighs and on the wall and feeling both hugely relieved and really fucking embarrassed at the same time.

I wake up with a gasp and realise with no small amount of dismay that I've just made a mess.

Shit.

Just then, the false dawn of the compound starts—they keep us on a twenty-four hour clock even though there's only a thirteen-hour rotation on this blasted hell of a planet—and it's already oh-five and Sarge is staring down at me from his cot with this *look* on his face when he sees what's on my stomach. Disappointment. Fuck, if he was angry, it would be better, but he's damn disappointed. I can see it in the air around him, like a dull-green, heavy fog, so I keep my hands to either side of me and try not to sound like I'm making excuses.

"Was a dream," I say, all low and ashamed. My voice actually cuts out at *dream*, so I sort of whisper the word. "Sorry, Sarge."

I see him go from let down to amused. He gives me a smile. I'm so fucking relieved that I can feel it like a tightness in my chest.

"What are you?" he laughs. "A damn weakling? Only weaklings can't control themselves in dreams, son."

"Y'sir," I mumble, feeling like an utter failure.

"Well, it's *no goddamn excuse*, Murph. I told you that you weren't given leave to touch that cock of yours," he says, sitting up. He rolls his shoulders back and, for a second, I can see through his skin the metal struts that he's never bothered to have replaced—an old method of repairing vaporized bone. That was from his first tour, before I was even born. You could chart the progress of technology by looking at Sarge's scars.

For a second I'm about to retort that I didn't actually touch my dick, but I just keep my trap shut.

"Come here," he says to me softly.

I sit up quickly and kneel in front of the bed. I've got my hands clutched behind my back and my head down. He hasn't told me to clean up, so I just watch the cum inch slowly down my belly, adding to the mess in my pubic hair.

"I want to punish you," he says softly, and it's all I can do not to let out the little moan that's sitting there in my throat. Instead I give a grunt and nod, and wonder what he's got in mind.

"Over my lap, son," he continues. I think I hesitate for a half second before complying, simply because the thought of being over his knee makes me blink in astonishment. But I shake it off and climb up onto the bed to lie down across his lap, only too aware that I'm making a mess of the sheets and his shorts. It's a little awkward, given that I sort of tower over him, but I get into position quickly and take a few short little huffs of breath because it feels like my heart's gonna burst through my chest, it's thumping so hard. I close my eyes and wait.

At first he only strokes me softly, up the back of one thigh, over my ass and down the other cheek, like he's admiring me. I gotta say, the scrutiny's got me all self-conscious, and my cheeks feel like they're on fire. His hand's warmer than my skin— I've been lying on the cold floor after all—and the touch tickles slightly. My cock's doing the equivalent of rolling over in bed and rubbing its eyes, and I feel it like a hardening lump between us.

I'm so tense that when the interminable wait finally ends and his hand cracks against my naked skin, I let out a yell that, I think, surprises the both of us.

"Sorry," I mutter, just a deep grumble against the sheet I'm pressing my face to, and I hear him laugh above me. He doesn't say anything else though, just starts spanking me like I'm a five-year-old boy.

It doesn't really hurt, not at first, but as he smacks me harder and covers the same skin over and over, it starts to sting and I let out a grunt with every strike. My cock's now stiff as hell and poking into his thighs as he hits me, and I've got my hands balled up in the bedding, and, oh fuck, this... *This* is what I've wanted for so fucking long, and I'm straining against him, no longer holding back the low moans pouring from my throat. I sound so needy.

"Please," I manage to choke out eventually, "Sarge, please." I don't even know what the hell I'm begging for, but it sounds just right, and he obviously likes it because he hits me harder. Finally, with all the grinding and thrusting I'm doing against him as he lays into me, I'm approaching that sweet point again, and I start to get a little desperate.

"Sarge," I pant, "I wanna cum. Please." Ah yes... That's something to beg for. However, he stops hitting me immediately, and I feel dazed as he orders me to get off of him and take my position on the floor again. Chest heaving, I obey, my dick jutting like a fucking brick from my pubes, and watch him whip out his own to start fisting it like mad.

"Give you a goddamn reward for cumming all over yourself like a goddamn child?" he says, his face flushed. I know he's right. I don't deserve it. "But, since you took your punishment so well, you get a small reward."

"Thank you, Sarge," I say, humbled.

I have no shame left. I'm his. One hundred percent. Whatever he wants, he can have it.

"Good..." he huffs. The head of his cock is purple and wet as the foreskin slides back and forth over it. Sarge's knuckles are white, and I watch a clear drop fall from the slit onto the floor. Suddenly he lurches off the bed and pushes his cock against my lips, and I open my mouth quickly. With a groan, he sends a shot of cum down the back of my throat and another, painting bitter stripes on my tongue as he milks his cock into my mouth.

With a last throaty sigh, he pulls back and smiles.

I swallow down my mouthful—every drop—just like a good boy and smile back.

Sarge

This compound was supposed to be temporary. When the shit first hit the fan, we thought it would last three months... maybe half a year tops. But, after five long fucking years on this goddamn planet, everything is starting to fall down around our ears. The reason this is relevant to me right now is that the only goddamn lift that still works in Section Two is at the back of the fucking muni bay.

So, I make the grand detour to the elevator, and I'm thumbing the button to call it, when I look over at the transpo hangar and see a bunch of C-778 Ghost jockeys in boots 'n' utes laughing themselves hoarse over something. A blond kid I can't remember the name of starts miming tearing off his shirt before staggering around pretending to clobber the others, his mug all twisted up. He's doing *The Incredible Hulk*, I figure, until the boys see me, and their heels click together faster than you can spit. They're looking *really* fucking shamed as hell, and it dawns on me right then and there who the fuck they're laughing at.

Murphy.

I feel the blood in my veins start to boil, and I'm staring like I could fucking kill them just with my eyes. Watching Murphy on the battlefield is like being privy to a beautiful, goddamn work of art. Grace, deadly precision, not a wasted motion, not one damn *lick* of hesitation or fear; he's worth five of these fucking shitheels.

The lift opens behind me with a chirpy little chime, but I ignore it. I march over to them, feeling the need to adjust their way of thinking, and let a few minutes pass as I glare at each of them in turn until they're shaking in their goddamn boots. Somewhere in the back of my head I know just how much I'm overreacting. Christ, everyone thinks he's a big fucking idiot, and he does absolutely *nothing* to change their minds about it. All they see is the muscle and they fucking assume—

Shit, why the hell do I even care? The fact that I do makes me tense and being tense makes me madder than a kicked hornet's nest.

"Seein' as all y'all seem to be suffering from a bad case of *cranial fucking rectosis*, I think that the best goddamn cure would be a nice dose of double watch duty for the rest of the goddamn month," I bark at them. I see my spit hit Private Edwards in the face, and, so help me god, I'm disappointed when he doesn't flinch; I'm after blood.

I open my mouth to give them "viper" duty—clearing the trench around the compound of fucking legless, squirming nightmares that no one in their right mind would mistake for snakes—when a familiar figure steps out of the shadow and fixes me with a look of concern that cuts right through my anger.

"Be at watch posts five through nine at oh-four tomorrow. Understood?" I growl.

"Aye aye, sir!"

"Dismissed." The boys take off almost at a run, tails tucked between their legs.

I turn, feeling a little deflated and none too proud of myself, and watch Murphy walk towards me.

He's wearing a white T-shirt that's stretched too tight across his chest and the usual dun cammies tucked into black boots; just another Marine but larger than life. Yep, those goddamn shitheads have it all wrong. There's nothing ungainly or lumbering about my boy. He walks like a goddamn panther.

Without the straps of his armour, the tattoos on Murphy's arms come to life. With every ripple of muscle, you see hummingbirds, dragonflies, and beetles soaring through a sky of serene blue. Makes me feel homesick for a world I never goddamn knew. Fuck, maybe I ain't been getting enough sleep. What is it about this kid, out of all the others before him, that has me on edge like this?

A siren goes off outside, followed by a blast. Murphy's head turns quick, and I watch his eyes track something I can't see. His kaleidoscope vision... Colours that bloom across the landscape or streak through the air like a madman painting the sky. I remember the beauty of it, and there's a tight feeling in my chest.

"Gettin' bold," he mumbles, turning back to me. His bright-blue eyes pin me to the spot, and for a sec I just stare back at him.

"Didn't have to," Murphy says eventually, cocking his head towards the hallway down where the Casper pilots disappeared.

Of course I didn't have to, and I'm still a bit confused as to why I fucking did what I did, but then I see something in Murphy's face that makes me frown. He looks embarrassed. For some reason, it sets me off again.

"What the fuck are you looking at me like that for? If I want to ram some lessons down some fucking throats, it's my goddamn prerogative," I growl at him. "What makes you think that was about you? You think you're so fucking precious? Our arrangement doesn't give you goddamn leave to question my goddamn actions. You're just a place to park my cock. You get me, son?" As the words leave my mouth and slam into Murphy, I see the hurt in his eyes, but I can't stop the word vomit. I feel like I'm watching myself from far away. "In fact, get down on your fucking knees right now, Marine."

Murphy's expression is guarded as he drops to his knees immediately. Anyone can just walk around the corner, but I quickly pull open my pants and yank out my cock to start jerking it, and fuck me if I can't get it hard. I'm acting like a goddamn fool. After a few more useless strokes, feeling like I'm drowning in my own embarrassment, I jam my dick back in my shorts and turn around to punch the lift button again. The doors slide open right away, and I get in, doing up my pants and feeling like a fucking Grade-A bastard. I don't turn around until the doors close and the elevator starts to go down.

A weaker man would have hit the bottle, feeling the way I was feeling, but instead I hit the gym and kicked the shit out of three men half my age before I make my way to my quarters. It's shortly past lights-out even though that fucking sun is blazing like a wrathful eye outside; I'd burn my hand if I touched the goddamn wall. When I stop in front of the cheap, grey resin door to my room, I pause. Right below my name, in shiny black letters: Pfc. Andrew Murphy. I reach out and touch the M, tapping it lightly with a fingertip, like a little hoodoo to guarantee that he'll be there on the other side of the door when I open it.

When I walk into the room, the lights are off, but I see right away that Murphy's lying naked on the floor where he sleeps every night. He's wearing his helmet with the beam turned on, and he's got one arm behind his head, propping it up so he can squint at something in his hand. It's a book—a real goddamn paper book. I'm wondering where the hell he found it when I see that he's staring at me quietly with that same wary look on his face as before.

Without a word, I strip down to my shorts, and I step over him to lie down on my cot. The silence is like a goddamn press on my chest, and I rub my eyes, trying to ignore it. Tomorrow's another day. Maybe I won't act like such a fucking imbecile.

I hear a tiny click and Murph's helmet light shuts off. He shifts in the dark, just breathing softly. When he finally speaks up, his voice is close to me, like he's sitting up.

"What I do, Sarge?" It's barely a whisper. He sounds like a little boy.

Christ on a fucking cracker.

I've half a mind just to tell him to go the fuck to sleep, but I can't. His question makes me feel like an asshole.

Something occurs to me.

"What were you doing in the transpo hangar, private?" I ask, curious.

"Knew you were headed back down. Thought we'd walk together."

I don't think I've ever heard Murphy string so many words

together. I frown.

"How'd you know I was done in Sec Two?"

"Memorized your schedule, Sarge. Just in case y'ever needin' me."

Shit. His answers make me feel even worse. I close my eyes and let out a long sigh.

"Listen... You didn't do anything wrong, son. I was shit out of line, givin' you hell like that. Caught me off guard, is all." I'm hoping he doesn't ask me *why*. I don't know what I'd fucking say... hearing those boys make fun of him... Shit, they might as well have been insulting me direct. They were disrespecting something that I... ah, *fuck*... something that I hold in goddamn high regard.

I think back on my words and wince.

You're just a place to park my cock.

I swear to fucking Christ there's something wrong with my head.

"If you wanna keep on being the butt of their jokes, that's your goddamn right... I can't say I understand it. But," I say, "doesn't it bother you, Murphy?" I look over at him, though I can't see anything in the dark. He's probably got a wrinkle between his eyebrows, all serious; I think about his habit of licking his bottom lip, just the tip of his tongue to the scar there when he's mulling something over. Suddenly I've got a smile on my face. It's not one of those happy smiles though—it's the kind that hurts a little.

"Naw, Sarge," he says quietly. "I don't much care."

"Why not?" I press on.

"Just not important." His voice is just a low grumble, and I can hear him shift in place again. I wonder if he's up on his knees. "I'm here to serve 'n' fight. Do my duty. Do my best. Help win the goddamn war."

I nod to myself.

"Make you proud," he adds in a whisper, and there's that little pain in my chest again.

"You're a good kid," I tell him. "Of course I'm goddamn proud of you. Now... Go to sleep."

"Aye'sir," he says, and I hear him settle back down.

I grind my teeth together and close my eyes again. Sentimentality gets you killed in a goddamn war. I should get my head checked for letting this arrangement get... personal. I *should* nip this in the bud.

Instead, I open my damn mouth and say:

"Walk with me to Mess Hall in the morning."

After a moment, I hear his reply, and there's an unmistakable smile in his voice.

"Thank you, Sarge."

MURPHY

This is first time I go out since the day my unit got decimated in the trenches. I've obviously been cooped up too long; it's just a little recon, but I feel like I'm literally vibrating with excitement as I smear tan and brick-red paint on my face. Private Wood and Singh are coming with me, and I see that they're going through weapons check one more time before we head out. The former is a bit of a shithead, and the latter's on the squirrely side, but they're both competent Marines, and they obey my orders without question.

I think back to the night Sarge gave those Casper jockeys in the hangar a dressing-down, and I smile a little to myself as I pick up my double-duty rifle. I sling it over my shoulder with a nutsack of armour-piercing rounds—just in case we run into one of them big, thick-shelled things—and I give a nod to the boys before leading them out.

Yeah, Sarge was good and pissed at something. I haven't quite figured it out, to be honest. I felt stupid that he felt he had to stand up for me, like I was bringing his reputation down because of my own damn faults. Didn't explain why he was so angry... and embarrassed.

The blast of hot air that hits me when the doors open dries out my eyeballs immediately, and I blink a few times before lowering the visor on my helmet. We used to get goggles early on, but after a while they just stopped sending them with supplies. Can't understand the reasoning behind it. In fact, the last few shipments of supplies that reached us were sorta pitiful. The fight keeps moving further out, while we're still stuck slogging away on this hell of a planet. I wonder if they'll eventually just give up on us.

I peer at the trench and the narrow bridge that opens slowly over it when I touch the pad, and I lift my fist in the air to keep the boys back. When I can't see anything moving other than the heat ripples in the air, I drop my hand to signal that we're good to go.

This recon mission's a little on the risky side. We don't normally head out in full daylight, seeing as we're surrounded by MMFD—that's miles and miles of fucking desert—but I think brass is getting antsy. Someone in the monitor bay spotted what looked like an enemy base nearby, and we're just going to take a little look-see to make sure it isn't just some problem with the scout pods; they're so sandblasted that the video feed from them looks like grainy, old-timey black and white film. I take point and lead my men past the last beacon posts.

The plus side of that whole fucked-up encounter in Sec Two, however, is that I've been accompanying Sarge to his meals since, and he's started to give me tasks that he says are more suitable to what I got between my ears. Meaning, he thinks I'm an idiot for being happy enough just being a Ground Pounder. I can't really complain though. He's right. I'm enjoying sitting in on the meetings with our resident xenobiologists, taking notes in laymen's terms so Sarge'll be informed. It's also caused a lot of raised eyebrows and head-tilts when I open my mouth to ask for clarification:

"Would you say that corresponds with the *substantia nigra*?"

Yeah, I'm having a little fun with it.

We've been walking for over an hour. I've got Singh behind me and Woodsy watching our six as we follow the curve of a dune. My intel says that the base should be right over the next little hill, but I haven't seen anything resembling buildings yet. Then, just as I'm about to tell the boys to do a sweep, I see one of the little hover cars the enemy uses for ground transport come skimming along the sand. *Fuck.* We've barely got any cover here. The best we can hope for is that they pass by us on the west side where the dune's lip is a little higher.

"Down," I growl, hoping they'll hear me... and thank fuck

they do. So the boys and I hug the ground with our bellies and wait. I think it's our lucky day because the hover car goes right past us and continues over the sand without stopping. I quickly slap open the compartment on my thigh and grab my binoculars to watch the damn thing disappear as it rises over the next ridge.

"Shielding," I mutter. It gets my goddamn goat—as Sarge would say—that we're fighting against so much superior technology. There could be a base as big as a fucking city right in front of us, and we can't tell because we can't see through their shields. Our scout pod must have breached the perimeter and made it out unseen.

Or did they leave it unscathed on purpose, hoping we'd mount a full-scale attack? *Shit*. It might be a trap.

I lift my hand to get the attention of the others, and I pop open the panel on my left arm to disable the communicator and the transmitter that broadcasts my location and vital signs. Woodsy and Singh quickly do the same. If the enemy is expecting company, you can be damn sure they're monitoring for anything out of the ordinary, and I don't want to be taking any chances with them picking up our signals.

But... have we already been spotted? Are they just playing with us? Are they waiting to see if we're just the advance team? I curse under my breath, and lay my cheek on the hot sand, thinking. HQ will be wondering right now if we're dead or just gone stealth; I can see Sarge standing there with his fists on his hips, scowling at the monitor.

We need cover. Right now. Who knows whether they've seen us or not, but I'm not just going to lie here waiting to be discovered by another skimmer that passes too fucking close. I lift my head to take a three-sixty with my binoculars and spot a small smudge about a quarter klick east of our position. I tap the on-switch to magnify and see that it's one of those big fucking rocks that make me think of icebergs floating beneath a sea of red sand. I motion to the others that we're going to make for it and lead the way at a crouch. With our backs to the rock, we'll make it to sundown and hoof it back to HQ under cover of night.

Three hours later, the giant red sun is finally kissing the horizon, and I breathe a sigh of relief. I'm sick to death of listening to Woodsy's whispered jokes, half of them so speciesist that I want to hand him over to the enemy just for being an intolerant asshole. See, I don't have anything against the bastards we're fighting, other than the fact that they started this goddamn war. I like to think that somewhere in their base, there's a guy just like me with the same sort of likes and shit, wondering whether he's ever gonna make it home. They're a lot like us—hell, I'm sure there's an alien version of Private Woods sitting with his buddies right now, cracking jokes about stupid humans.

The one thing that's keeping me from throttling Woodsy's the fact that he's almost piss-his-pants scared. It's coming off of him in ice-blue waves. You know what they say: fear breeds intolerance... I sigh as he launches into yet another fucking joke.

I hear Singh's almost-silent double tongue-click and lift my hand to shut Woodsy up. I shift to the side and peer around the edge of the BFR. Singh points to something, and my heart goes double for a breath or two. There's a skimmer, not fifteen metres away from our hiding spot, just idling, and it seems there's something wrong with it judging from the panels the pilot has open. I hear Singh clear his throat, and I look back at him. He's got a huge, shit-eating grin as he lifts the flap on his side bag.

Inside, like eggs cozy in a nest, are five charge grenades. He points to the hover car and then in the direction of the shielded base, and I frown. Then it dawns on me what he might be thinking.

"Stickers?" I mouth, wondering if they're the type fitted with magnets.

He smiles wider and gives me a thumbs-up.

Like I said before, this guy's a little squirrely. I look back over at the skimmer and see that the pilot's closing up, done with his repairs.

I feel like telling him that his plan is stupid. It's ridiculous. It's fucking insane. The enemy can't possibly be that sloppy.

But you know what? Fuck it. I give Singh the OK and grab

Woodsy by a strap of his armour to drag him off a few feet. I quickly go through my compartments and come up with a tube of degreaser that I figure I won't miss. Woodsy gives me a look like I've lost my mind, but I mime throwing it and then point to the skimmer visible just beyond our cover. Woodsy's eyes get as big as fucking saucers, but I grab him again and give him a little shake before pointing to Singh who's crouched like a runner just behind the BFR. It'll be sunset in just a few minutes, and visibility is at its worst when the sun's just peeking above the sand. It's now or fucking never.

Knowing that Woodsy still has no fucking clue what we're doing, I throw the tube of degreaser as far as I can. Seriously, this feels like one of the dumbest, most amateur plans ever. There's no way the pilot will be stupid enough to fall for it. However, I see his head turn when the tube hits the sand just north of where he's standing. When Woodsy follows my lead and throws something that lands with a heavier thud, the pilot takes a few steps forward, scanning ahead.

Quick as a wink and silent as a shadow, Singh runs and dives under the skimmer. In seconds he's done and races back for cover just as the pilot decides he's just hearing things. I'm almost laughing at this point.

The three of us watch him climb back into the little hover car and take off towards the hidden base. They've probably got scanners to detect foreign objects. Especially dangerous objects like five 10-ton blast-bombs, stuck like limpets to the undercarriage of a vehicle entering the base.

Singh holds three fingers up as he watches the countdown on his wrist cuff.

Two fingers. I'm holding my breath as I see the skimmer disappear beyond the shielding.

One finger. Woodsy, having finally caught on, is muttering, c'mon c'mon c'mon, under his breath.

With a theatrical loop of his arm to mime tossing a grenade, Singh marks the end of the countdown, and to my utter and total amazement... The charges go off.

The sky above the hidden base erupts in an eye searingly bright explosion of fire seconds before the base itself flickers into view as the shielding fails. Fireballs burst out of buildings, signalling secondary blasts as the conflagration spreads, and the black cloud blots out the last of the dying sunlight. Either the base was filled with numbskulls, or we just got really fucking lucky.

Singh's laughing like a crazy man while Woodsy lets out a whoop and does this funny little shuffling dance. Me? I'm just grinning like a fucking idiot. I chuckle a little to myself and shake my head before starting off at a jog towards HQ.

"C'mon," I yell over my shoulder. "Fucker's are gonna be lookin' for us."

Singh and Woodsy catch up to either side of me as we hoof it double-time back to base. The excitement and amazement at what we pulled off is such a bright haze around us that I'm sort of sad that I'm the only one who sees it.

MURPHY

Someone thrusts another beer into my hand, and I get patted on the back, but whoever it was is gone before I can say my thanks. We're heroes. Tonight, anyway. I pop the tab and take a sip of the lukewarm brew as I look around. The men are all laughing and talking, trading insults and coming up with theories about how we pulled it off. Lance Corporal Jameson walks up to me and punches me hard in the arm before giving me one of her crooked smiles. She's always been sort of nice to me, and I smile back before she melts back into the crowd. Even the Casper pilots give me little nods as they pass by. It's bizarre, and I'm a little overwhelmed, to be honest. Not that I haven't been called out for being heroic—I have. A few times now. But seeing as we're down to less than a hundred men... I don't know. It feels more... significant.

I scan the faces around me, looking for one in particular, and I'm worried when I don't see him. Apart from when we made it back to HQ, sunburned and sandblasted, panting and laughing like imbeciles, I haven't seen Sarge. I down the beer in a few gulps and crush the can before chucking it at Woodsy's head. It hits him, not hard mind you, and he flips me the bird. He's drunk.

Without saying goodbye to anyone, I push my way through the crowd to the double doors of the mess hall and make my escape.

The first place I check is the gym, but it's completely empty. Same with the locker room. I figure maybe he's in our quarters, so I head up B corridor towards barracks; but, as I'm passing one of the big monitor stations, I smell burning tobacco and stop.

There, standing in front of the window looking out at the dark desert wasteland, is Sarge.

For a second I wonder if I should just head back to the party, thinking he could be wanting some peace and quiet, but I must have made a noise because he turns his head and fixes me with a stare. I take a few steps into the room and see that he's smoking one of his cigars. While that might seem like a normal thing to do on a celebratory night such as this, I know right away something's wrong. He treasures those things. Has maybe four of them left... and that's not a happy smile he greets me with.

Sarge is angry. And more.

I drop to my knees beside him and put my chin to chest. I hear a burning crackle as he sucks on the cigar, and I wait. After a moment he lets out a sigh.

"You turned off your goddamn transmitter."

I blink a few times.

"Y'sir."

"You were in such a fucking hurry you couldn't signal your intent to HQ? What kind of a goddamn fucking amateur do you have to be to go black without letting anyone know? We thought you were dead."

He's being unfair. He knows that I did what I did because I felt we were in immediate danger. But I know why he's angry now, and it feels like there's a hollow space in my gut where my stomach should be.

I lift my head and see that he's gone back to staring out the window. On an impulse, I reach for his hand. He turns to watch me, his thick brows low over brown eyes darkened to black in the dim light of the room. I press my forehead to his knuckles.

He thought I was dead. I feel ashamed that I made him worry. Ashamed... and touched.

"I'm sorry." For a second I worry that maybe he feels humiliated by me holding his hand like this, but when he pulls it out of my grasp to touch the top of my head softly, I breathe a sigh of relief.

He stubs out the cigar and leaves the room, and I know I'm

supposed to follow. When we get to our quarters, he stands next to the cot just staring up at me. I have no idea what I'm supposed to do, so I stand there awkwardly for a second wondering if I should get back down on my knees.

Finally he says something.

"Get undressed."

My pulse starts to race as I tug my T-shirt up and over my head. He's reaching into his pants for his cock as I work loose the buckle on my belt and tug down my zipper. I'm already half-hard by the time I've kicked off my boots and left my clothes in a pile on the floor.

Sarge is stroking that thick, curved cock of his while his gaze slides down my body so slowly I swear I can feel it on my skin. I know he finds me nice looking enough, but it makes my heart thunder and my prick swell knowing he's getting hard just looking at me.

He pulls his own clothes off, almost distractedly, and I realize suddenly that I've never seen him completely naked before. He's in great shape, but age is starting to show in the tiny slackness of his skin here and there as he moves. I suddenly feel so young in comparison. Out of my league. My face feels hot as he takes another slow look at me.

"On the bed."

I move to comply, unsure how he wants me to sit or lie down, but he puts out a hand to push me down on my back, settling the question. I watch him grab a bottle of lube from the rickety nightstand and pump a few squirts into his hand. I'm almost panting from nerves, wanting so much to please him. He lubes up his cock until it's glossy then grabs mine to stroke it slowly a few times. It feels so good I'm almost whimpering. But then he lets go of my dick to shove my legs apart and up, and before I have a chance to think about what's happening, his cock is pushing into me.

I feel him slide the rest of the way, a hard thing inside me that stretches me open, and I let out a small, pained grunt. He starts to fuck me, and my body loosens bit by bit as I get used to it.

My cock starts to go soft. If I'm honest, I have to say that I've never really enjoyed being fucked. I always thought that since I'm a sub I'd love it, but the experience is always just a little bit unpleasant. However, this is Sarge, and if he wants to fuck me, he gets to fuck me. My hands are twisted in the sheets to either side of me, and I let out little huffs of breath every time he goes balls-deep, like I'm loving it.

His chest starts to shine with sweat as he continues to plough me, obviously enjoying himself. Then, he gets this little furrow in his brow as he's watching my face and slows to a stop. I wonder for a second if I did something wrong, but he just moves forward so he's leaning over me. With the strangest expression, he slides a hand under my head and slowly, almost like he's testing something, he presses his lips to mine. I feel like I've just stepped off a cliff with no chute. When he nudges his tongue almost shyly against my bottom lip, I open my mouth and let him kiss me deep.

It's a rough kiss. Neither of us is much practiced in the art, but we press into each other like we've been dying for this very moment. He starts fucking me again with short little slow thrusts and I don't know if it's the change in angle or the kissing, but it starts to feel good. Really good. My cock hardens on my belly, and I start groaning into his mouth.

Sarge finally breaks the kiss and pulls out. I figure he's going to cum on my chest like he likes to, but he coaxes me onto my hands and knees to fuck me some more. The change in position's a little disappointing at first, it doesn't feel the same, but then he reaches beneath me to grab my cock and starts to jerk me off. Now I'm straining back against him with every thrust, completely eager.

With a low grunt, Sarge's hand stops suddenly, and I realise almost in shock that he's cumming inside me.

With a moan, I curl my fist around his, and I stroke his hand quickly over my cock. I'm so lost in the moment that it doesn't even occur to me to ask if I can climax, but then he leans against me, kisses my back, and murmurs:

"Cum for me. Cum like a good boy."

Between the thought of Sarge filling my ass and those goddamn words, that's all it takes.

With a cry I let loose and feel like I'm drowning the bed in a week's worth of spunk. It's gotta be the best orgasm I've ever had. A toe-curling explosion that ends with me panting and making these whimpery little sounds as my cock twitches and jerks in his hand, his dick still deep in my ass.

Sarge pulls out after I'm done. My thighs are shaking so bad I don't know if I can stand, but when he says a quiet, "Come on," I nearly fall off the bed as I move to obey. He tosses me a white towel before he opens the door, and I stagger after him in a daze, wrapping it around my hips. The hallways are empty; everyone is still partying. Sarge takes us up a level, and I'm a little confused, but when I see we're heading for the officers' showers, I understand.

Like everywhere else, it's deserted. We pass through the locker room into an open, white-tiled shower area sectioned off by white resin dividers. Then, he grabs my towel and throws it into the pile on the floor with his before reaching for the faucet.

I think I literally groan when the water touches my skin. It's a little cooler than what we get down in the general shower area, and it feels fucking fantastic. I open my eyes and see that Sarge is smiling at me a little. I know I'm making a bit of a fool of myself, but I can't help it. It's like my whole body's been craving water. We're allowed a grand total of five minutes of water a week. Otherwise, we use the dry showers, which don't come anywhere near to satisfying one's needs.

Officers don't have a water limit.

Sarge steps under the spray with me and we touch. It's a little awkward at first—like neither of us knows what we're doing—but then he reaches up and pulls my head down to continue the kiss we started earlier.

At least six weeks of water rations pour down on us as we make out like boys in the shower. When Sarge pulls away and shuts off the water, I feel a pang, not ready for it to stop. However, he just grabs the soap and starts to wash me all over like I'm a little kid. Well... A little kid whose cock gets a bit plump as Sarge slides his hands over it.

"Kneel," he says to me. His voice sounds odd. "Please."

I wonder if we're going to fuck again in the shower, but when I get down on the tiles, he just continues to soap me, massaging my neck and my shoulders, then my scalp. I thought I loved the man before... But that feeling *pales* in comparison to the one that's making it so hard for me to breathe right now.

I close my eyes as he washes me gently like I'm the most important thing in the fucking world.

SARGE

After all the damage caused by enemy retaliation, this goddamn compound is no longer sufficiently keeping us safe from the goddamn elements. There's a pile of sand in the hallway. It blew in through a big hole punched into the side of the building, and I kick it as I make my way back from the temporary War Room. We've lost electricity in over half the base at this point, so we're holding all tactical meetings in the mess hall for the time being.

It's a fucking gong show.

Murphy walks next to me, his long legs easily keeping up with my quick strides. He's been the only thing keeping me from a fucking meltdown for the last few weeks as we spiral further into dire straits. Top brass won't listen to my recommendation that we pull out ASAFP. They're also not convinced that sending us some back-up is "the best course of action at this time". I swear I could fucking murder someone with my bare hands.

I'm not a patient man. No, my skills lie elsewhere. Murphy, in comparison, is like a still lake. When I look over at him and meet those clear-blue eyes of his, I know he can tell I'm raging; I can't hide anything from him, not when he can see it like hot steam rising out of my head.

We have to get off this fucking planet, and we can't afford to lose any more goddamn men, that's for fucking sure.

"Last push, Sarge," says Murphy, his deep voice quiet and full of concern.

"Last push, my ass. Fucking 'last push' was three weeks ago. We're not even beating a dead horse, we *are* the goddamn dead horse."

Murphy frowns and doesn't answer, which is probably a damn good thing.

I yank open the door to our quarters and throw my pad at my desk, not caring that it glances off the fake wood and crashes to the floor. Probably another goddamn thing broken now.

Murphy stands in the middle of the room, looking around him, a thoughtful expression on his face. I'm tempted to take out my frustrations on him, fuck him hard enough to hurt and then cum in his face... but truth is that I'm burned out.

"Sit." He says it like he's distracted. I think it's the first time I've ever heard him tell me to do something. Part of me is irritated by it, but mostly I'm too tired to care. I sit down on the edge of the cot and watch him sort through his belongings. After a few minutes he finds something in his kit and smiles.

Murphy holds out his hand. Sitting in his palm is a set of neuro-relays like the one we used before. Shit, it might even be the same ones.

"What are those for?"

He comes towards me and kneels in front of me, like he usually does. But then he reaches up and presses the relay to the side of my head, right where it sat the last time. Don't know why I don't even try to stop him.

After he presses the other relay to his own head, the lights begin to twinkle as they fall into sync.

I blink and my world turns into a crazy mess of colours.

I hear a harsh whine from the failing A/C and look up to see the noise like a slash of red across my vision. My heart starts drumming in my ears, and I feel my palms go sweaty. I'm quickly getting nauseous from the visual onslaught, and I'm about to pull the relay off, when Murphy reaches up to take my hands. I turn back to him, breathing real fast through my nose, and see his pupils shrink. He's watching me carefully, and there are slow waves of different hues coming from him, but I can't make goddamn heads or tails of it. Fuck, it wasn't this *intense* last time. Maybe it was the hubba. Maybe it was shock.

"Just relax," he says with a little smile.

He can see my panic.

I'm embarrassed about panicking.

Shit. He can see I'm embarrassed.

"Relax," he repeats.

"What is the goddamn point of this exercise?" I growl.

"For fun."

"You're so fucking wordy, you know that? Jesus H particular Christ, I don't understand why you'd think this was fucking *fun.*"

A new colour blends with the others around him. A soft red. Almost pink.

"What is—Are you *amused* by this?" I accuse him.

Murphy grins wide.

"Y'sir."

I look down when I realise he's stroking the backs of my hands with this thumbs. It's soothing. I take a deep breath.

"So that's what that means? Pink is amused?" I ask, frowning at him. I gotta admit, I'm interested. The dizzy, stoned feeling starts to fade.

He just shrugs like I'm mostly right.

I notice that some of the other colours, the colder ones, are melting away like fog. Is it because he's less worried now?

"Goddamn it, how do you make sense of all this?" I'm exasperated.

Murphy shrugs again.

"Born with it."

His answer does nothing but make me more frustrated. But, somewhere buried in that... I'm awed.

The air around Murphy is a deeper hue now, still soft, but growing bolder, and he looks so serious. He lifts one of my hands to his face and turns it over. With his bright-blue eyes on mine, he *very* slowly and deliberately licks my palm, his soft tongue flat and gentle. It's so fucking intimate and unexpected that I let out a tiny, involuntary groan and see the colours around Murphy bloom wild. His pupils expand, and he bites the heel of my hand with a smile.

He is beautiful. So goddamn beautiful.

I run my fingertips against his lips, coaxing them open before I slide two fingers into his warm, wet mouth. Murphy shuts his eyes and sucks on them softly. His tongue works its way between them, and I make another sound.

For the first time, I think I'm seeing exactly just how much this means to him. The air is almost vibrating, shot through with colours I can't even begin to name as I stroke the back of his neck with the other hand, then over his shoulder and down his chest. Taking his nipple between my fingers I squeeze gently, and then harder. I don't hear the noise he makes, but I feel it on the fingers that slide further down the cradle of his tongue. Then, when I pinch him hard enough to hurt, I see what has to be pain erupt like a jagged flower before it's completely swallowed by more pleasure.

Murphy is utterly naked, body and soul, and I can't get him onto the cot fast enough.

He's on his back, straining up against me, my cock in his hand, his in mine, as I bite hard on his shoulder. I smile when I'm rewarded with a weak groan. I can keep this up forever, I think. I'm fine-tuning his reactions, coaxing more and more out of him as I figure out what he likes the most. I can feel him shaking against me as I keep up a steady flow of words, most of it murmured straight into his ear as I jerk him off slowly.

"...uh-uh, I feel you fucking my hand like a bad boy. Didn't I tell you to keep still while I pump this goddamn pretty cock of yours? Heh... There... That feels nice, doesn't it? Look how easy it is to make your dick all nice and wet and slippery... How long has it been since I let you cum? Two weeks? Ahh, that's a long time, isn't it? It's because I want to hear you beg for it like a greedy little boy. But, before you're allowed to empty those big balls of yours, I wanna fuck that tight ass of yours... feel your hot little hole squeeze my cock..."

Murphy lets out what could only be called a whimper when I shift away out of his grasp and manoeuvre myself between those thick, muscled thighs of his, the head of my cock slick and swollen against his pucker. He closes his eyes with a frown as I ease in slowly.

"Just relax and take my dick like a good boy, Murphy. That's it. Alllll the way... nice and deep. Oof, Christ, you feel fucking great, you know that?" I start fucking him—long strokes that have my balls slapping against him as I push myself hard into his body, my hands around his ankles, holding his legs up and knees back to open him up to my thrusts. I'm already getting close. It's unbelievable how tight he is; he's like a goddamn virgin.

Falling forward on my fists, my cock going like a greased piston, I see that Murphy's starting to enjoy this—the smears of colours around him are throbbing in time to my fucking, and he starts moaning *please please please* in this gorgeous goddamn desperate voice. Then, his forehead wrinkles and, with such a raw, frantic look in his eyes, pupils blown out to hell, he reaches for my head with one of those huge hands of his and pulls me down, his mouth open to mine and hips shifting to meet every stroke. I'm grunting like a goddamn beast as I plough him harder, and I can't remember the last time I felt this... *alive*. Shit, I feel like a kid again.

Somewhere I wonder whether I'm getting more than just Murphy's colour-vision... Maybe I'm a little inside his head, and he's inside mine.

I reach between us to grab Murphy's big, rock-solid dick, and I start to stroke him, sweat and precum making it so damn slick. In almost no time, he makes a noise like he's startled, and his hands grab hold of me tight, his ass pulsing on my cock as he pulls his face away to let out a cry. With a groan, I press my face hard against his shoulder, fucking into him deep a last few times to push myself to the very edge.

Oh fuck, I'm going to cum.

I pull out quick and get up on my knees, cock in fist. Murphy's chest and stomach are covered in pearly white streaks where he came all over himself, some of it dripping down over his ribs as he looks up at me, panting and wide-eyed, watching me jerk off over him.

It's a fucking gorgeous sight.

I give a growl and finally let go, cumming all over his wet

cock and adding to the seed running down his heaving belly. The pleasure crashes through me, spurt by thick spurt as I choke and milk my cock, ending on a long groan. Then, legs shaking like crazy, I sit back on my heels to catch my breath. With one hand, I stroke the inside of Murphy's wet thigh gently.

"Thank you." Trust Murphy to know exactly what I needed.

He closes his eyes and nods once. I can't help but think that using relays like this for too long has to cause some sort of damage, but right now I couldn't care less.

There's something coming off Murphy in waves that I want to watch for a little longer.

SARGE

I adjust the strap on my helmet and frown. I haven't worn this goddamn thing since I got shot. It feels... weird. I look up and see that Murphy's tightening the webbing across his chest, every movement of his hands practiced and efficient. He's so concentrated on what he's doing that when he sees me watching him, he doesn't even acknowledge me. I look down at my own armour and yank the collar closed. I'm dressed from neck to ankle in black, flexible nano-shielding. I'm already hot as hell, but we're headed underground, so I probably won't sweat to death. Still, I glance over at Murph with his straps 'n' shells—as the grunts call their chopped armour—and can't help but be a little envious.

When he's done, Murphy reaches for my shoulder without a word and adjusts the fit of the chest plate I've got on. He's over a head taller than me, and I feel weirdly like a kid when he just turns me around to tighten the strap that runs across my back. I'm glad we're alone right now. *No one* helps me to suit up. Self-sufficiency is a good goddamn model for the men, and I like to show them that I'm not one of those milquetoast officers who have to have their asses wiped for them.

Something about Murphy's touch is too possessive, too confident. He's taking liberties with me, assuming I want his help, and it makes me tense, so I shove his hand away. He looks at me with that quiet, deep calm he's always got going on, and I just want to fucking rip into him.

He thinks I'm on edge because we're being sent on what I think is a fucking suicide mission; it's such a misuse of resources that it's fucking criminal.

Thing is, he's completely right, and I realize suddenly that helping me with my gear is probably a way of putting his own mind at ease. I figure I owe him that much.

I square my shoulders and take a deep breath. After a sec, I give him a little nod to continue, and he comes forward again, doing something to my chinstrap. Right away, my helmet is already sitting better on my head. I watch him as he quickly fixes me up so that everything fits comfortably like a second skin.

Murphy's not just a *resource*.

There are flecks of silver in those bright-blue eyes... serene eyes. He smells like the paint he has smeared like big bruises on his face, but beneath that I can smell *him*: musky, a little sweaty, and something that instantly brings to mind the taste of his skin between my teeth. I think I've finally figured out what the word *cherish* means. His gaze shifts to mine, like he can tell what I'm thinking, but he just steps back and gives me one of his brief nods.

"Ready, Sarge?"

"Ready, son."

It's a little past sunup by the time the team gets to the mouth of the cave. I signal to Lance and Gomez to stay back and guard the entrance, and then I lead the others into the cool tunnel. One by one, helmet lights come on, and when we get to the first fork, everyone stops. I pull out the plastic map from the Velcroed pouch at my forearm and peer at it.

Two weeks ago, satellites with geothermal cameras spotted this series of tunnels. Then some squinter noticed signs of activity on the surface a few klicks from here. Assuming that it's another shielded base, this cave system passes right beneath it. Our mission is to make our way through these goddamn tunnels to plant enough TNT to blow the fucking thing sky-high.

Regardless of the outcome, we get to go home after this. There's an extraction team on its way as we speak. We're to rendezvous with them at the other end of the cave network. HQ is deserted; everyone is with me for the last push. The very *last* of the last pushes or, as Murphy has taken to calling it, *Operation*

Dead Horse. Problem is, the squinters calculated a sixty-seven-point-four-five percent probability that the enemy uses these tunnels themselves. Which means, it's going to be an underground fucking firefight, our backs to the walls, if that turns out to be true.

I point to Singh and motion for him to scout ahead down the right-hand fork. He nods and takes off quickly down the tunnel. I glance to the side and see that Murphy's looking down the left fork with a deep frown on his face.

"What is it, private?" I ask softly.

"Maybe nothin', sir," he replies after a tiny pause, but whatever it is has his hackles up. I hear Singh's soft whistle and signal the team forward. I can't help but notice that Murph throws another look at that dark opening before falling into line.

It's all gone to hell.

The air crackles around me as Adams sends another charge blast down the tunnel. We can still hear Singh screaming from wherever he was dragged to. It's a fucking maze down here with blind tunnels and pitfalls everywhere you look. We're completely lost. We've been lost since we stepped foot in this goddamn cave system. My map is more than useless, and something is jamming comms. Couldn't raise anyone if I fucking tried.

I hear another hum of electricity as Su, the xenobiologist, finally gets his BFG turned back on. The kid's never seen combat... He's been flying a desk his whole goddamn career. We're down to six men. *Six* men out of a team of eighteen.

Jameson lets out a shriek as her side explodes in a shower of blood and bone fragments, and she's dead before she even hits the ground. We're up against intelligent grenades that hover and hone in on body heat. You can't even see the fucking things because they're shielded.

Now we're down to five.

There's a spray of rock near the mouth of the widest tunnel, and I can hear that Murphy's switched to using armour-piercing rounds. See, we're not even up against the enemy... just their goddamn booby traps, but the local wildlife has also come out to play.

Then I hear a noise that I never want to hear again in my goddamn life; Murphy's howls of pain cut into me like a knife, and I race down the tunnel.

I can hear Su screaming as he lets charge after charge go off behind him as he follows me. My boot catches on a rock, and I pitch headfirst into the smooth tunnel wall. Something makes a loud popping noise, and there's a gurgle. I turn around to see that Su's literally lost his head. It takes a half second before his body realises it's dead and crumbles to the ground. Had I not stumbled, that might have been me that took the stealth grenade.

Murphy's quiet now. I can't see for shit with the curves of the tunnel, and I go between cursing and praying as I brace myself for what I might find.

Finally, I see the light from Murphy's helmet. It's not moving, and at first I assume the worst, but I hear a hiss of breath and turn my head. He's propped up against the wall, panting. He seems uninjured until I notice that he's sitting in a circle of red and one of those big, muscled legs of his just ends about mid-thigh. Quickly, I smack open the panel on my chest, pulling out and dropping supplies behind me as I run forward. My heart's going faster than hell when my fingers finally close on the corner of the sealant bandage. I yank it out and, as fast as I can, I get it unwrapped and unfolded, dropping to my knees in the spreading blood puddle. I press it against his stump to stop the life from pumping out of him in huge spurts with every beat of his big heart.

I get the edges sealed and I take a shaky breath. He's almost gulping his air, his system in shock, and I grab his head between my hands.

"It's gonna be OK, son. Are you hurt anywhere else?"

His eyes finally focus on me, but he looks completely dazed. In the cold light of the beam coming from my helmet, he looks pale as a ghost beneath the dirt and blood and paint. Slowly, he shakes his head.

I fumble some more through my med-kit for a pin-sticker of HeBA and quickly jam it into his neck. I do a little math in my head and give him a second dose just in case. I watch the drug take effect, and though Murphy's still panting like he's run a race, the lines of his face soften. He looks like he's going to pass out. I glance around to get a better idea of our surroundings, and that's when I notice the huge hulk of the dead thing blocking the other end of the tunnel. Murphy's missing leg is sticking out from under it. I let out a laugh that sounds a little unhinged.

"You had to go and take on one of those by yourself, didn't you? Too proud to ask for some goddamn help?" I joke, but when I turn back to Murphy, I see that he's closed his eyes.

There's a deep rumble right then, and I feel the ground beneath us shake. Rock dust sifts down from the ceiling, coating the pool of blood in a layer of white. Murphy coughs a little.

"Explosives."

A second rumble, closer this time, makes the tunnel shake again.

"Must be the ones Singh was carrying," I reply.

Murphy's really quiet, and I reach out to touch his neck... looking for a pulse. He grabs my hand, his eyes opening slowly. His lips quirk into a tired smile.

"Know what'd be nice?" he asks. His voice is just a low rasp.

"Anything."

"A little water."

I laugh like a goddamn idiot as I grab the canteen from my hip and pull it free. Murphy takes it from me, but when he only fumbles at it, I take it back and slide open the top for him and lift it to his lips. He takes a few long swallows, some leaking down over his chin making streaks in the rock dust that covers his face.

"Thanks, Sarge," he says and leans his head back against the wall. I realize a second later that he's shaking. He's lost so much fucking blood...

I get up, grab him by his shoulder straps, and haul him across the floor, out of the cold, gory puddle. Then I sit down on the ground and pull him backwards onto me. I curl my arms around him, wondering what the fuck we're going to do. He's too big. I can't carry him. I don't even know where the fuck we are... and any moment someone's going to come around the corner and finish us off.

"Anybody live?" he mumbles. His lips are too pale.

"I don't know. Su is dead. Adams too. We might be the last ones left."

"Should go, Sarge." He says it so quiet I can barely hear him.

"The fuck I will."

We sit there in the near dark. The only sound is his ragged breathing... The battle beyond has gone silent. I wonder about the explosions again.

"M'sorry."

"What are you sorry about?" I fold his arms over his chest and wrap my hands around his. His skin is like ice.

"Dunno." Murphy opens his eyes and looks up at me. "Just. Sorry."

"Listen to me you foolish, goddamn boy... There's nothing for you to be fucking sorry about."

He smiles, but it's barely on his lips before his eyelids slip closed again.

"You're not allowed to go," I growl into his ear. "Do you hear me, Marine? That's a fucking order!" He doesn't move, and I tighten my hold on him. "Answer me, goddamn it! Who the fuck is going to spit-shine my boots if you go? Goddamn it, Andrew, don't you fucking go." I can barely feel his pulse.

It's like there's a deep chasm inside me.

I hear a noise. Someone's coming up the tunnel. Fuck, I just want a few minutes... Just another few fucking minutes. Is that too much to ask? I don't want to leave him. I don't want him to be alone when he goes.

"Casper."

My heart trips and winds up halfway up my goddamn throat.

Murphy cracks one eye open briefly; thank god he's still with me. Then what he said registers with me. *Casper.*

Sure enough, a second later the comm bead in my ear suddenly comes to life, and I hear the unmistakable humming whine of a C-778 Ghost's engines in the background as an unfamiliar voice speaks.

"Sergeant Wilkes? Do you copy?"

"Fuck yes," I laugh into the mic. I must sound like a madman.

"We'll have you dug out in a jiff, sir. I can see your coordinates on my screen, and there are four men coming to you directly up the tunnel to your east. I don't want you to shoot them."

"Halle-fucking-lujah," I say. "I want off this fucking rock."

The woman laughs.

"Yessir. We're your ticket home."

Home.

Never has a word made me happier. I tell her about the stealth grenades, and she relays the information to the extraction team. Turns out that they have new scanners that detect them. I think about my men, their bodies littering the caves, and grind my teeth.

But now's not the time to be angry.

"Please hurry," I say to the woman high above us, "I've got a man here who's critical… and I have a personal stake in his survival."

"Understood, sir. Just hold tight. Everything will be all right."

I squeeze Murphy's cold hand and press my forehead to his. When he squeezes my hand back weakly, I close my eyes in thanks to whatever powers that be.

"We're going to make it, Murph. We're going home."

murphy

BEY DECKARD

For those that think it's too late.

MURPHY

I swing my legs over the side of the bed but pause a sec before putting my weight on the right one. The doc thinks I'm imagining things. He says that all the little servos are ready when I am, but I swear to god there's a lag when I first wake up—enough that I've almost wound up kissing the deck a few times. If it keeps happening, I'm going to ask to see someone else in Bionics. Maybe there's something wrong with the calibration. I'm hoping it's that and not brain damage caused by the cheap neuro-relays Sarge and I use from time to time. Brain damage is reparable, sure... but sometimes you're just not the same afterwards.

When I'm satisfied that my leg's awake, I stand up and give my back and shoulders a quick stretch. My muscles are sore from being tied up for so long yesterday, but it's not so bad. At least my nuts don't hurt anymore... That's something.

I grin.

There are towels in a little locker by the door, and I grab one to sling around my hips before I make my way to the officers' showers.

It's not far, but every uniformed PFC and LCpl salutes me along the way, something that makes me feel a touch uncomfortable. Naw, it's not because I'm parading around in a towel that doesn't even make it to mid-thigh—I'm just not used to my rank yet. I keep telling myself that it's no big deal. Shit, I just heard about another guy who was recently bumped from private first class to sergeant in one shot like I was. Maybe all you need to get to NCO these days is to cheat death and not fuck up while doing it. Nothing special about that.

Still, when the guys look up and salute me—me in my tiny towel and shiny metal leg tromping down the narrow passageway like some fucked up, sweaty cyborg—I can't help but feel like I don't really deserve it. All I did was lose a leg and survive.

I duck into the big shower room, happy to have the space to myself for the moment, and pick a private stall at the end. It's nice that I'm reasonably well liked by the men now that they've figured out I'm no idiot, but sometimes I miss the old days. Lately, it feels like I don't get a whole lot of time to myself.

I turn on the shower, then brace myself against the bulkhead with my hands, stepping back to angle myself forward so the water falls over my shoulders. Damn showerheads barely come up to my chin.

I can't help but let out a little moan at how nice the heat feels soaking into my sore muscles. There's no shortage of hot water on the ship, so I stand there for a full glorious ten minutes before I start to soap myself up.

As I'm rinsing off, I hear a group come in. Through the divider I see the rosy glow of their collective good mood, and I smile to myself when they start horsing around a bit. Spirits are high since reports of the latest victory. Maybe we'll win this damn war after all.

I can only place a few voices, but that's not surprising. We just picked up two other squads in the last week, and I wonder if they're meant to accompany us F.I.S.T.S. to the final destination.

The Federated InterStellar Tactical Squad™—or F.I.S.T.S. for short—is the squadron that Sarge was given after we brought down the enemy base so spectacularly three months ago, and it's mostly made up of us lucky fuckers that survived *Operation Dead Horse*.

You know, when I woke up and found Singh hooked up to the Casper's ICU next to me, I honestly thought he was dead. It's a damn miracle he survived. Our squirrely explosives expert lost an eye, part of his nose, and his right arm, and all that kept him from being lunch was the stealth mine that went off and killed the thing eating him. Then, all chewed up and skin dissolving with digestive acids, Singh picked himself up—crazy fucker that he is—

and made his way to the blast target to set the charges before he got the fuck out of there.

He got three medals. I'd say they're well earned.

Lance and Gomez were supposed to double-time it to the rendezvous point from where they'd been left guarding the tunnel's entrance. Unfortunately for them, once the charges went off, the enemy came boiling out of the base like it was an anthill on fire, and they ran smack into the mess. Lance was KIA, but Gomez got pulled out of there by the extraction team with only a few charge burns.

In addition to the four of us, we've also got a few new squad members: a recently promoted staff sergeant named Rudyck who seems all right, a couple of trigger-pullers from some Sino-Russian colony I'd never heard of, and an expert that will join us in just over two weeks.

I'm thinking about what I read in this expert's dossier as I reach for the shower knob to turn it off, but I stop myself when I realize that I've become the topic of conversation outside the stall.

"Yeah, I dunno. How do you get your men to pay you any respect if they know that you're basically your commanding officer's cock-holster?" The voice is female and not one that I recognize.

"Jesus, Sam! What is this? The forties?" laughs another voice, and I smile. It's Gunnery Sergeant James Khouri; he's well respected by the men, myself included. "You realize I could bring you in front of Ethics just for using the term *cock-holster*, don't you?"

"Jim, seriously, when was the last time you heard of someone *actually* getting to see an Ethics Counsellor? I still think top brass canned them all to save on budget." I hear her laugh and watch the hues coming from that way become sort of muddled. When she speaks again, she sounds a little contrite. "Shit, I didn't mean it in the *gay* sense—I'm not an asshole. It's just the weird sex-slave thing I keep hearing about."

There's a round of awkward laughter and some cringeworthy speculation. Marines with nothing to do between missions are the worst when it comes to scuttlebutt. When the chatter dies down a little, a familiar voice speaks up.

"You know, I saw them at it once."

I frown—that sounds like Rudyck. I wonder what the hell he's talking about when the air around me colours over in curiosity and shocked amusement as he goes into his story. I feel my face burn. There's no mistaking it: Rudyck saw Sarge and me in the botanics bay a few weeks ago. I was obviously distracted enough by what Sarge was doing to me to have missed the man's presence.

Stupid. I take back what I said about Rudyck being all right.

"And let me guess... You were standing there for that long because you were hoping to join in?"

The whole group erupts in laughter at Khouri's interruption of Rudyck's enthusiastic account. The air is streaked with the jagged hues of embarrassment. I press my forehead against the cool wall and close my eyes. Well... shit... That's what we get for being so indiscreet.

Khouri's voice rises above the noise.

"Why don't you mind your own business, Matthew? Listen, I know Murphy... In the line of duty, the man's as loyal and self-sacrificing as they come. I admire that. If he wants to obey Wilkes the same way in private, then I say Wilkes is a damn lucky man."

I'm extremely thankful for Khouri's words, and I figure that's the end of it when no one speaks for a bit, but then I almost groan out loud at what comes next.

"Just seems like a shame, no?" The voice sounds familiar, but no name comes to mind right away. "I mean, have you *seen* the size of the cock on him? Fuck, I'm not even a bit gay, and I want to get a better look at it. Shit, if he never gets to, uh"—the man's laughter is breathy and nervous—"you know, actually *use* it... Well, it's a damn waste! Right? Rudyck, did you see it get hard? How big was it? I figure it's gotta be at least as big as my wrist when... it's..." He trails off as I quickly turn off the water and step out of the stall before he can say anything else. I've had enough of this.

All eyes are on me, but it's steamed up enough in the room that I'm hoping no one realizes how red my face is. Though I can see they're as embarrassed as I am, it's me that has to pass them to get to the exit, so I give a polite little nod and try to act cool as I half-assedly towel myself off while walking. Then, out of nowhere comes this stupid impulse, and as I step past Brisbane—the asshole going on about my dick—I mutter, "Nah, it's bigger," just loud enough for him to hear. Then I'm out of the showers and through the locker room as calmly as I can manage it.

As I'm walking back to my quarters with a hand over the swelling, embarrassment-fuelled boner that's trying to rip the towel from around my hips, I can't help but laugh at myself. What's wrong with me?

I open the door, and Sarge looks up from the pad he's reading. I wasn't expecting him to be back yet, and I freeze in place, my heart knocking away at my ribs while he takes a good long look at what I'm trying to hide.

"Come in and shut the door," he says real quiet, and I obey. My face burns hotter as his eyes drill into me. With a grim little smile, he reaches out to pull my hand away, and the towel falls to the floor, unmasking my source of shame.

"Well, well, well... What the fuck's got you so damn worked up, son?" he says, and flicks the head of my cock hard; I wince but manage not to make a sound. "Have you been a bad boy and touched something that doesn't belong to you? And don't you goddamn lie to me." He's so close that I can see the faint scar around his eye socket. The colours pulsing from him are rich and dark. It's hard to breathe.

Technically, I haven't done a thing wrong... but...

I just give a single nod and Sarge smiles.

SARGE

There's something real goddamn weird about this mission. I can't put my finger on it, but you develop a highly tuned sense for bureaucratic bullcrap after so many years in uniform. And this? This stinks to high heaven. I still don't have much in the way of details aside from what's called a "blind budget" from our backers. I'm mulling over the abridged and wholly fucking obfuscated list I've been given, wondering how common this shit was before the military was privatized—history's never been one of my strong points—when there's a knock on the door.

I nod to Murphy, and he gets to his feet to answer it. On the other side is Staff Sergeant Matthew Rudyck looking like he'd rather be anywhere else in the galaxy than standing in Murphy's shadow.

"Well?" I ask. My mood's only going south. "What do you want, Rudyck?"

"I... You asked to see me, Master Sergeant?"

Shit. Where is my goddamn head?

"Of course I did!" I growl at him. "Murphy, out of the goddamn way, and let him in." Murphy's eyes meet mine, briefly, before he turns away from the door and goes back to the cot where his book is. The spine's creased like it's been read a thousand times, and I can barely make out the title: *The Death Ship.*

I think about sending Murphy out of the room, but... Shit, I can't help it. It's stupid, but I want him to see this.

Rudyck stands easy in front of me, hands clasped behind him and feet shoulders'-width apart. He's nervous, but he ain't nervous enough, and it has me grinding my teeth as I'm staring daggers into him. I'm none too pleased to have been spied on by this pissant, and from what Murphy said, Rudyck got quite the eyeful. Serves me right for not being able to keep my cock out of Murphy's mouth for very long.

The word *addiction* comes to mind. I clear my throat.

"You're off the mission."

Rudyck's eyebrows jump like they're trying to get away from him.

"Sir?"

"Was I mumbling, Rudyck?"

"No, sir. I... I—"

"The next words out of your mouth, so help me god, better be 'I know I am grossly unsuited for any goddamn *top secret* mission because I am burdened with the inability to keep *my goddamn trap shut.*' "

Rudyck takes two quick breaths through his nose before answering me. Yeah, he knows *exactly* what I'm getting at.

"Yes, sir. I'm sorry, sir."

"You're off the squad indefinitely. In fact, I've asked to have you transferred to... ah..." Murphy's in my line of sight, so I see it when he looks up at me. His expression is thoughtful. There's no reproach, just quiet, keen intelligence in those serene eyes. I suddenly feel petty in comparison and decide right then not to send Rudyck to the deep freeze like I'd intended. "Another ship," I finish lamely. "You'll be assigned to something more suitable to your expertise. *Dismissed.*" I just want him out of the fucking room.

Rudyck snaps me a salute even though private rooms are categorized as "indoors" on the old starcruiser.

"Thank you, sir." He knows he got off easy.

When the door closes after him, I turn to Murphy. He's gone back to his book, but though his eyes are moving, I get the sense that all his attention is focused on me.

"Well?"

A smile tugs at the corner of his mouth, dimpling his cheek, and he glances up.

"Thanks, Sarge," he says. I catch a hint of amusement buried in the gravel of his voice.

I shake my head. He's not thanking me for the display, that's for shit sure.

"That kid deserves to freeze his ass off with a spell of deep space watch duty... You're goddamn soft, you know that?" I grumble and give my face a rub. "And you're making *me* goddamn soft."

As his grin gets a little wider, I'm struck with just how much trouble I'm in. My career has always come first. *Always.* What the hell are you supposed to do when something else becomes more important?

I turn my back on the gorgeous boy sitting on the bed, and I awkwardly grab for a pair of shorts.

"Going to the gym."

"Sarge."

I have to look at him because of something I hear in his voice. Murphy's still slouched on his side with his back up against the wall and one elbow dug into the mattress. He's wearing a white T-shirt with a worn-out pair of navy pants that look like they came from an old C-99 Horus flight suit, and he's barefoot. He looks rumpled and relaxed stretched out on the bed, and there's a gentle sort of confidence in his expression as he stares up at me.

"I'll come with."

Like hell, you will. I clench my fist tighter around the black shorts. No, I just need to get away for a bit. Shake him out of my system. Get back to what's *important*.

"All right," I say instead. "Grab your shit and let's go." I watch him mark his place in the book before sliding off the bed to put it carefully away in the little corner unit. As he bends over to grab his workout gear, I shake my head. That perfect ass...

Yeah, who the fuck am I kidding? I can't hide anything from him—I want him with me, and I'm glad as hell that he's joining me. That's the damn truth.

A vigorous workout and a quick shower afterwards has us back to the room about an hour later. We're getting dressed for the evening meal, and I'm slipping my belt through the loops in my blue dress pants when Murphy stops what he's doing to watch me. I lift an eyebrow at him and wonder what's going through his head. He just smiles a little shyly, and without a word, he leans in and those soft lips of his find mine in an open-mouth kiss that has me almost embarrassed by how fast it has my heart going. With his chest hair still shower-damp and skin smelling faintly of soap, he's a rock-solid, warm presence against me. I taste a hint of toothpaste on his lips as I quest out for something deeper, but he's away again just as suddenly. In a sort of daze, I watch him do up the tiny buttons of his white shirt, and his face gets a little flushed from the scrutiny. I can still feel him right there, under my goddamn skin.

"What the hell was that for?" I ask, making my voice gruff. My pulse is still speeding merrily along.

Murphy just glances at me out of the corner of his eye and lifts one shoulder up in a shrug as he finishes buttoning his shirt, but I'm not fooled one bit.

Jesus, I am in a *shit-ton* of trouble.

"Ok, quit looking so proud of yourself," I growl.

Murphy's face splits into a smile. I know we're going to be late for supper but...

"Come here, boy, and do that again."

SARGE

It's a quiet oh-dark-thirty as I'm impatiently swiping through the latest mission parameters on my pad—Christ only knows why, considering I ain't fucking privy to half the goddamned details—when I see the little bootlicker assigned to this guard shift pop up like a prairie dog from his seat and look over sorta nervously at me in my cell. At the entrance to the brig, I see the familiar mouse-brown high 'n' tight of Sergeant Andrew Murphy, and for a sec, it's like my smile is trying to take over my whole goddamn face.

The guard stands rigidly at attention and barks out:

"Sir, Private Machado reports post number B3 all secure. Post and orders remain the same. Nothing unusual to report."

Murphy nods, and I hear his rumble of dismissal. Quick as a wink, Machado hightails it out of there, happy to be let loose early. As Murphy gets closer, I see that his usual graceful stride is a tad stiff, and I feel my heart rate kick up a notch because I know it doesn't have a goddamn thing to do with that new leg of his. Nah, it just means he's been a good boy, and knowing what he's got on under his uniform has me tugging at the crotch of my blues as I get up off the bench.

"Master Sergeant," he says and stands at attention, fists at his sides and eyes forward.

"Well, aren't you a fucking sight for sore eyes," I reply. Murphy's punctual as all hell, but I like to play as if he's been keeping me waiting. His bright blue gaze flicks to mine, and his forehead wrinkles up as his face gets a little pink. He's gorgeous, my boy.

"Sorry, Sarge." His voice is so low I barely hear it. An apology offered with no questions and no excuses... Just the way I like it.

"So you came to bust me out of jail, son?"

"Y'sir." I make the same fucking lame joke every goddamn time—there's something about seeing him again after a stretch that makes my mouth stupid—but Murphy smiles that quiet smile of his anyway.

See, along with my new rank, I was slapped with a six-year jail sentence for a seven-one-oh-eight-bravo-slash-six—*improper disposal of weapons within enemy territory*—but it was reduced to thirteen weeks on a technicality, and because of the stepped-up timetable of the next offensive, I'm able to serve it out a day and a half at a time when duty allows. At this rate, I'll be in my nineties by the time I've finished this goddamn sentence, but looking at the boy standing perfectly at attention outside my cell, I'd say it was fucking worth it... Thirty-six hours never seemed so fucking *long* before.

My impatience blatant as all hell to him, Murphy glances at his watch and gives a little headshake. We've got some time to kill. With a sigh I cross my arms, careful not to brush the charge screen—one touch feels like being slammed upside the head by a short iron—and then nod towards the dark-grey cammies he's got on. The bulge in the front of his pants is bordering on obscene.

"Show me."

Murphy's eyes widen a touch, and deep wrinkles stripe his forehead again. I watch his tongue come out to tease the scar in his lip before he glances over his shoulder, and I frown. Ever since he found out about that dogfucker Rudyck watching us, Murphy's got a touch of the jitters. He's got nothing to worry about right now though. I made damn sure of it.

"Are you really going to make me repeat myself?"

"N'sir."

Without another second of hesitation, Murphy yanks his T-shirt out of his pants and pulls it over his head with a clinking of dog tags. In addition to the tattoos that cover his arms to the knuckle, he's now got a slew of blurred-edge fractals across his chest. The shapes shift with the flexing of his muscles as he quickly gets to work on his pants, and damn if the colours don't remind me of the ones he sees.

Murphy's expression is softly shy as he folds down the waist of his cammies and exposes the narrow leather belt that sits right above his hips. He swallows, and then slowly pulls the pants lower, revealing another strap going down the front. The way he's drawing it out means that he's either putting on a little show for me—which ain't his style—or he's feeling a mite tender. It's right then that I realize what I mistook for part of the dark camo pattern on his pants is in fact a big damp spot over his crotch. As the material parts, his dick surges forward, head swollen and slick. Trapped snug behind the balls by the thick padded ring set into the strap of the harness, Murphy's cock looks harder than hell.

As he lets his pants drop past his knees, I feel my own dick throb hard; the material tightens over my thigh, and I have to clear my throat before speaking.

"Jesus, Murph. That's a goddamn sight"—I watch a clear drop stretch from the tip of his cock to break free and land in the cammies that are puddled around his ankles, and I tug again at my crotch to relieve the strain some, laughing all quiet-like—"but that ain't what I was asking to see."

Just before Murphy turns around, I catch a glimpse of the burn in his face, and that sends another pulse straight to my fucking groin. Immediately, he drops to his knees with a clang and goes forward onto his fists to present his ass to me. There's a narrow strap that runs down from the belt at his waist to the oblong base of the plug buried deep inside him. As he moves his hips back and up a touch, spreading his knees, I can see the strap between the padded cock ring and the plug's base. I exhale hard; the leather is soaked through.

"Oh Christ, you *have* been good. Goddamn, that is be-*yoo*-tiful, son." I can't stop myself; I nearly rip the button from my pants in my hurry to free my cock. We've got another minute or so to go before the electrified barrier of my cell will turn off, and I'm eager as hell. Like I said: thirty-six hours is a goddamn bitch. I groan and run my fist slowly over my shaft. I can see that Murphy's cock is now linked to the textured steel deck by a long string of precum.

"Will you just look at the mess you've made of yourself? How long's your cock been drooling all over you?"

"All day, Sarge. Like you wanted."

I get an image of Murphy going about his day with the plug nestled inside him, holding him open, like a goddamn placeholder for my cock. The thought makes me jerk my dick faster. I'm almost panting.

"But..." Murphy looks over his shoulder at me, and his eyes lock on my hand as I stroke myself. I squeeze my shaft right behind the head. A drop of precum beads out, and he licks his lips, eager goddamn cocksucker that he is.

"What is it, son? Speak up."

"Had to take it out a couple times," he confesses, lifting his gaze.

"Why?"

"Needed more lube, and"—his voice drops lower—"needed a break. I just... really thought I was going to jizz in my pants."

I grin at the look on his face. He looks so horny and ashamed at the same time... Yeah, that's my boy.

"Take it out for me now." I was aiming for a growl, but it ends up sounding a little choked.

Murphy reaches behind him and fumbles at the buckle holding the strap to the waist belt. It comes loose, and as he faces forward again, he digs his fingers under the edge of the plug's base and starts to pull on it. I can see his pucker stretched tight around the neck of the plug, skin bulging out a bit before the thing slides out of him all black and shiny. His asshole stays gaped for a tantalizing second, and all I can think about is getting my cock in him ASAFP.

"*Shit.*" I have to stop jerking off, or I'm going to hit the charge field with a whole fuckload of cum any second. "That's good." I'm breathing hard as I squeeze the base of my shaft. I close my eyes. My hands are shaking, and Murphy makes a soft sound, just a little moan. Oh yeah, he knows what's coming.

There's nothing but a whiff of ozone and a happy little chime to let me know that the field keeping me trapped in my cell is gone, but it might as well have been a starter pistol. I stagger forward, and I'm barely on my knees before I slam my cock into Murphy's ass. I hear his pained cry, but he stays his ground, even pushing back into my onslaught as I curl my hand around the waist strap of the harness. It's five thrusts, maybe less, before I let loose with a cry of my own and pump his hole full of cum.

I wait until I've got my wind back and pull out, squeezing the last few dribbles out of my dick. Murphy's asshole is all gorgeous and sloppy, and I use my thumb to push some of the mess into him before I grab the plug to stop him up. He lets out a whimper as it slides in tight, and he starts shaking a bit as I rebuckle the strap. I give him a second before I help him to his feet. There's a tiny little groan that escapes through his clenched teeth with every breath he takes, and I swear to fucking god, there's a tear in his eye.

There ain't a single thing in this whole goddamn universe more beautiful to me.

When he reaches down to grab his pants to pull them up, he sways a little. I watch him drag the material up over his leaking, rock-hard dick and gingerly zip himself in with a pained hiss. Then he bends down to grab his white T-shirt and uses it to clean up the little clear puddle he left behind on the deck. I smile.

"Good boy."

He balls the shirt up in one big mitt and shuts his eyes, breathing deep. I let another couple seconds go by so he can get a hold of himself.

"Good boy." This time I say it a little quieter. Gentle. When he opens up those baby blues and shines them on me, my chest hurts so bad that I have to clench my teeth against the pain. I reach up and wrap my hand around the back of his neck and give it a squeeze.

The smile Murphy gives me brings back the ache for a second, and for the millionth time, I thank whatever the fuck it was that put us in each other's path.

MURPHY

We make rendezvous with the ancient galaxy-class transport in good time. It might seem a ridiculous waste of fuel to bring one man so far out to this quadrant, but seeing as our squad's mission is top-level classified, brass decided that the specifics of it had to be relayed in person—there's a damn good chance that the enemy's cracked our encryption again, and the folks up top really don't want them to know what we got planned. I have to say I'm damn curious myself.

Right now, I'm standing in pod bay three, just waiting for the ship to finish docking. Since Sarge is needed elsewhere, I've been made the welcoming committee. Thing is, I feel inadequately prepared because I don't even know the expert's name. The only thing his dossier contained was a list of his specialties and the commendations he's received over the course of what seems like a long career.

I hear the outer hatch clang and the warning chimes that precede pressurization, so I straighten my shoulders out and fix my stance so that I'm rigidly at attention.

The LEDs on the inner hatch go from red to green right before it opens. I'm a little surprised by the fact that the man is in mufti, and I wonder for a moment whether I'm supposed to salute him.

Fuck it.

I give him a neat salute, fingers coming to rest on the brim of my utility cover, and he stops and returns it.

"At ease."

"Good morning, sir," I say. "Welcome aboard the *FSC Kartikeya.*"

"Morning? It's evening for me," he replies with a grimace. He's almost as tall as I am, but where I'm built like a brick shithouse—as Sarge likes to say—the man standing in front of me brings to mind a stick insect. However, he's got lively blue eyes under brows that are almost black in comparison to his silver buzz cut, and all I can read from him is curiosity and friendly intent.

"Sergeant Andrew Murphy," I say in introduction.

"Ah, you're the big fella I keep hearing about. It's nice to meet you, and congratulations on your promotion." His teeth are white and even beneath his brushy little grey moustache. "I'm Second Lieutenant Oliver Grunwalt, but everyone just calls me Ollie." He grins wider at the look on my face—see, I was under the impression that Sarge would be the commanding officer on this mission—but he obviously mistakes the reason behind my surprise. "Relax, Sergeant. I like things a little informal. No need for the spit-and-polish routine."

I let out a small grunt and nod. I think of pointing out that our Master Sergeant lets the men call him *Sarge*, but instead I just give him a friendly enough smile.

"Murphy," is what I offer him. Ollie laughs and claps me on the shoulder.

"All right, Murphy," he says, hefting his seabag, "I'd like a little shut-eye before meeting with Wilkes. Can you show me to my bunk?"

"Aye'sir."

As we walk the passageway, the lieutenant keeps up a steady chatter, mostly about the quality of the food on the old transpo ship. Curiosity about the upcoming mission is sort of gnawing at me, but I refrain from asking him, seeing as he hasn't met with Sarge yet. I can wait. But, when we get to his assigned room, Ollie turns to me with a grin.

"Trust me when I say this isn't just some boondoggle, Murphy." He strokes his moustache down with a little chuckle. The man just exudes good humour, but... I dunno... There's just something keeping me from letting my guard down. "Tell me: what's your experience with swamps?"

A few hours later, I'm standing in line to get my inoculations while trying to ignore the fact that Brisbane is up ahead and keeps twisting his neck to look back at me.

Not even a bit gay, my ass.

The line's slow as hell because two of the auto-meds are still busted, and it looks like one of the bigger squads is readying up for something. Finally Brisbane gets his shot, but the fucker slows as he passes by me, and he gives me another go over. It's nearly a leer, and I'm sort of kicking myself for goading him the way I did. Live and learn, right?

At long last, it's my turn. I step up onto the weighing plate and hold my tags in front of the electronic eye so the auto-med can read them and pull up what mission I'm assigned to. There's a *blip*, and the arm cuff extends from the unit. I squeeze my bicep into it, warm still from the previous guy, and wait. On the small readout, there's a scrolling list of side effects I could suffer next to the percentage in my demographic who experienced them:

nausea 22%, fever 21%, vomiting and/or diarrhoea 9%, rash 0.9%, temporary blindness 0.3%, heart failure 0.004%...

"Yeah yeah," I mutter at it. "Just get on with it." I've probably had over fifty vaccinations in my life—there isn't a disease or virus we can't cure or protect against—but I've only reacted negatively to a handful. I'm impatient because Sarge is in conference until sixteen hundred, and I'm to meet him in our quarters immediately after. At this speed, I'm going to be late.

Shit.

Finally the auto-med decides that I'm ready and sends the shot through my skin. It doesn't hurt, but it's not exactly pleasant either. Then I have to stand there for a second while it checks my vitals. After a *bleep* the unit wishes me a good day and the pressure on the cuff is reduced enough that I can yank my arm out of it. My watch says I have eleven minutes to get from one end of the ship to the other. It'll take a fucking miracle to get to Sarge on time.

I'm on deck eight when the first wave of nausea crashes into me, and I grab the guardrail and just hang on tight while I wait for the feeling to pass. It takes about five long minutes before I can continue on my way without wanting to hurl my guts out, but by then I'm shivering and there's this ache in my bones. I have to concentrate on keeping one foot ahead of the other, but I'm getting motion sick just from walking.

I have to rest again on deck seven, and when I get to deck six where the officers' quarters are, I feel like utter and complete shit. Hell, even my hair hurts.

The door's right there, but it takes me two tries before I'm able to open it. I almost collapse into the room.

"Where the fuck have you been?" growls Sarge when he sees me stagger in. I stand there swaying and swallowing. There's pressure in my ears muffling his words.

"Med bay," I say and rub a hand over my face like I'm clearing cobwebs from my eyes.

"When I said I wanted you here at sixteen hundred, I didn't mean sixteen-oh-one, I didn't mean sixteen-oh-five, and"—Sarge looks at his watch—"I sure as *shit* did not mean *sixteen-twenty-two*. Where in the hell do you get off wandering in here as you fucking please... and looking like a bag of smashed asshole to fucking boot? What do you have to say for yourself, Marine?"

"Sorry... uh..." My eyeballs are throbbing.

Sarge reaches for his belt and starts to unbuckle it as he takes a step towards me.

"Get on your fucking knees!" he barks out, sounding madder than hell. I feel another swell of nausea and swallow hard. The words just won't form in my mouth, so I'm standing there like a dumb shit staring at him. "Are you fucking deaf? Get. On. Your. Knees."

Oh god. Just the thought of sucking cock right now is going to make me puke. I press my lips together and give a little headshake.

Sarge goes still, his eyes searing into me.

"No?" he asks.

"No." It's just a whisper, but at the sound of it, the outrage on his face blinks out like a light. What it's replaced by is a wide look of concern. The air is almost crackling around him, and I wince. The vivid hues hurt my eyes.

"What's wrong?" Then he remembers where I said I was. "Vaccine?"

I nod, sending the world spinning again. It's all I can do to stay on my feet.

Shaking his head, Sarge grabs me by the arm and steers me towards the double-wide cot against the back wall.

"Get the fuck in bed... *Now*." It's a low growl, and I can't help but smile at the ferocity behind it. I stumble the last few steps and crash down on the bed gratefully, shivering as Sarge pulls the scratchy ersatz-wool blanket over me. He disappears for half a minute or so, and when he gets back, he presses something to my neck before draping a cool cloth over my forehead.

"Need to get that fever down," he mutters. When he notices I'm watching him, my eyes half-lidded, he sucks on his teeth and shakes his head. "Go to sleep."

It's another order, one that I am only too glad to follow. I manage another weak smile and close my eyes thankfully. Sarge rests his hand on my head all gentle for a moment, the contact soothing, and then I hear him walk away and settle into the nearby chair. As I'm drowsing to the sound of him cursing under his breath over the reports he hates doing so much, something occurs to me: did I stumble because of the reaction to the vaccine, or is my leg malfunctioning again? However, it's not long before sleep chases all thoughts away.

I open my eyes. The room is completely dark, and apart from the subdued feedback I constantly get from the ship's engines, everything is still and quiet. When I move my head against the pillow, I feel the pull of something on my neck, and my fingers recognize it as a dermal patch. That's when the memory of earlier comes flooding back. Thankfully, I think the fever's gone...

I feel ok. A quick tap to my watch shows me that it's just past oh-three-hundred. I've been asleep almost eleven hours.

There's a soft noise behind me, and I feel Sarge's hand snake over my hip. I'm naked, but I'm pretty sure I passed out fully clothed.

"Feeling better?" It's a sleepy mumble, and it makes me grin.

"Y'sir," I reply.

"You weigh a fucking ton, Murphy. Almost broke my goddamn back getting you stripped after your fever broke."

"Sorry, Sarge." I've only got a vague recollection. Mostly of him swearing.

He just lets out a quiet laugh and then presses his forehead to the back of my neck.

"I'll punish you for it in the morning."

Now it's my turn to laugh.

"Aye'sir."

MURPHY

Ten hours until we reach our destination, and the level of excitement aboard the *Kartikeya* is off the charts. This mission is supposed to be big. Problem is, no one actually knows *what* it is. Everything is hush-hush, but there's a lot of speculation. Some are saying that the enemy's home world has been discovered, and that's where we're headed. I don't think that's it. Second Lieutenant Grunwalt is sharing command with Sarge over the F.I.S.T.S. and a few hand-chosen members of another squad—twelve men in all. That's not nearly enough for an effective planet-side offensive, especially with no heavy gunners on the roster. But maybe there are others joining us. Who knows?

The fact that everyone is so keyed up is starting to get to me. It shouldn't... I'm used to pre-mission jitters. Maybe the added stress I'm feeling has to do with the fact that, for a few nerve-wracking seconds this morning, my leg wouldn't budge. It's too late to see anyone about it now, but if we're successful and I come back in one piece, well you can be damn sure that Bionics is going to be my first stop. I haven't said anything to Sarge. I don't want to be taken off the mission—I belong at his side.

Thing is, Sarge *has* noticed that I'm a touch tense, so he has me working it out.

My muscles are starting to shake as I start yet another set of reps. Knuckles to steel, sweat running down my arms, I let myself down and then quickly push back up with a quiet grunt. Sarge is standing over me, arms crossed, just watching. As I do another press-up, I wonder how long he's going to have me doing this.

Five, six...

I'm past where I usually stop. It's not the muscle fatigue or the pain—that, I can take for a while longer. No, what *usually* has me stopping two sets ago is the fear of getting off in my shorts while in a crowded gym. Not sure why, but when I get to a certain point, whether pull-ups or press-ups, my dick gets hard. From then on, it's like every rep starts getting me closer, and not only because of the friction. Used to freak me out when it first started, but as it turns out, it's not that uncommon. I think it happens more often to women, but guys experience it too. I guess I'm one of the lucky ones, if you want to call it luck.

Eleven, twelve…

I figure it has something to do with clenching certain muscles, but at the moment it's made worse by my naked cock sliding into the slick puddle I'm leaving behind on the deck with every rep. I'm having a hard time concentrating on being good.

Fourteen, fifteen…

My next press-up ends on a groan. I've let myself cum this way a few times, and let me tell you, it's fucking fantastic. Right now though, I'm not supposed to blow my load without permission. At this rate, I'm not going to make it to twenty.

Shit… Seventeen, eighteen…

My eyes are screwed up tight, and I'm panting through my teeth. Don't wanna disappoint Sarge.

Argh fuck… Nineteen…

I feel a tiny pulse and my cock jerks. I'm too damn close, so I just lie there, a big trembling mess. A few seconds tick by, and I get kicked lightly in the side.

"Did you forget how to count, Marine?" growls Sarge.

"N'sir," I whisper. I can do my last rep and cover the deck in spunk, or I can grovel.

I choose the latter.

Sarge's foot digs into my ribs, and I wrap myself around it, pressing my lips to the black leather of his boot, hoping to appease him. I've got my knees almost up to my chin, curled up tight like a pill bug. Sarge lets out a quiet chuckle.

"Well… Why did you stop?" he asks me.

I shiver, squeezing my eyes even tighter. Then I take a deep breath and answer.

"Was gonna cum without your say-so, Sarge," I say in a low, shamed voice.

There's that laugh again, and he untangles his leg from my grasp. He walks away, and I hear him sit down on the bed. Breathing slowly to calm myself, I listen to him unlace his boots and kick them off. The *burr* of his zipper is followed by the soft sounds of cloth falling to the deck.

I open my eyes and lift my head. Sarge is naked and sitting back on the bed with his legs spread. His cock's not hard yet, but it's throbbing to full as I watch.

"Come."

I'm on my feet and up on the bed quickly. I've still got a raging hard-on, but the moment of respite on the cold steel has pulled me back from the edge. Without being asked, I crawl between Sarge's legs and take him into my mouth. I don't need to hear his pleased noise to know that he's happy with me. I can see it in the air around us. I allow myself a small, inward grin.

"That's right, Murphy. You suck my goddamn cock," he says, pushing my head down so that my nose touches his greying short 'n' curlies. I tighten my lips but relax my throat, savouring the feeling for a moment before pulling back to suck him down again. Soon, he grabs hold and starts to buck up, forcing me to work at a furious, throat-bruising pace.

"Oh goddamn yes," murmurs Sarge. "*Fuck* yes. You like it when I fuck your mouth, eh, boy? Oh you love the taste of cock, don't you? Let me hear you say it..." He pushes back on my head, pulling his dick out of my mouth to smack my lips with it.

"Y'sir."

"Yes, sir, w*hat?*"

"Yes, I love the taste of cock, sir," I choke out and lick precum off my lips.

He laughs all low and thrusts himself back into my mouth to fuck it to the back of my throat a few more times. However, he lets out a gasp and grabs for his shaft only a few strokes later. I pull away, knowing that he's close.

"Shit." He's panting and red-faced when I glance up. A trickle of sweat makes its way down between his pecs. I duck my head and begin bathing his balls softly with my tongue, waiting until he asks for my mouth again. The skin of his sack is wrinkled tight, and as I lap at it, Sarge lets out a soft groan. I carefully ease his balls into my mouth, gentle the way he likes, and work my tongue around them for a little bit. He bends his knees to give me better access, and I grab the back of his thighs to push them up even more.

With my nose full of his clean, musky smell, I run my tongue lower down to circle his pucker. I'm rewarded with a sigh of encouragement. Slowly I tongue into his ass, just light licks at first, then far enough that I feel his sphincter's ring throbbing tight around my tongue. Above me, he's started to jerk himself again at a lazy pace, urging me on with whispers and light touches to my head.

"Oh, yeah. Eat that ass, son," he says. "*Jesus*, that's fucking good..."

I pause to suck on his hole, like I'm going to give it a hickey. Sarge loves it when I do that; he growls a little then moans as I push my tongue back into him as deep as I can. His hips are moving slightly with my tongue fucking, and I'm trying hard to keep myself from humping the mattress beneath me.

I'm back to teasing around his hole again, just wondering what he would do if I decided to try a finger, when he shoves me away. It only confuses me for a second because when he climbs off the bed and starts to try to drag me to the edge, I know exactly what he wants. I flip onto my back and wriggle so that my head hangs off the mattress. Almost immediately Sarge shoves the head of his dick past my lips and halfway down my throat. I rarely even have to suppress a gag in this position; I just close my eyes and breathe when I'm given the chance.

"That's it. Open *real* wide," growls Sarge, burying my face in his crotch. With a grunt he forces my lips up around the base of his cock, impaling me. "Oh *Christ*, I love watching you take it all in like a good boy." He pulls back, and I take a gulp of air and cough.

"You're probably dying to play with that big prick of yours, aren't you, son?" He slaps my cheek hard, and I open my eyes.

"Y'sir."

"Well, go on then." He smiles down at me and swipes at my bottom lip with his thumb.

"Thanks, Sarge." I sound hoarse and needy, and I let out a groan as I close my fist around my hard, leaking cock. It won't take much... But then again, I know it won't take much for Sarge either. I only hope he'll let me cum this time.

Or do I?

Sarge starts fucking my mouth again, deep thrusts that have his nuts smacking against my face. He's grunting like a beast, barely letting me have time to breathe. I have to slow my hand or else I'm going to lose control.

"Ahh... fuck! Oh, you're not even gonna *taste* my cum, son. No, I'm gonna send it straight... down... your... oof... fucking throa—*fuck*!"

His cock swells in my mouth, almost causing me to gag as he shoots his load. I squeeze my dick hard. I haven't been given permission to release... but now it's too late. Muffled by the cock lodged in my throat, I barely make a noise as I cover my chest and belly with spurt after spurt. He releases me, and I cry out a hoarse sob, stroking my dick as it lets loose with yet another jet of cum into the cooling mess puddling on my skin—for a long moment, I'm senseless to anything but the bursting, throbbing crescendo that has me straining and shuddering on the thin mattress.

Finally it recedes, and I'm panting like I ran a fucking marathon as my body goes limp. I shift so my head's on the bed, and when I hazard a look at Sarge, I see that his nostrils are slightly flared and his brow is furrowed.

But, thankfully, it looks like I have nothing to worry about.

"You made a goddamn mess," he says. He's amused.

"Mmmyessir." My lips are numb and the back of my throat is burning, but I'm just... *floating*. I close my eyes again.

The mattress sinks with Sarge's weight as he sits down next

to me.

"I oughta tan your ass."

I smile and nod.

"You're something else, Murph," he says, and I open my eyes at the tiny catch in his voice.

Words can never do justice to this, so I don't even try.

SARGE

I'm trying to get suited up, but I can't keep my eyes off of Murphy as he's attempting to fit into his protective gear. The way it's hugging him is almost goddamn pornographic.

The world we're orbiting is wet. *Real* fucking wet. It's 99 percent ocean, and the only continent on it is a patch of brackish swampland that covers just about seventy million hectares. We're to be dropped somewhere in the middle of it, and that means we're going to get wet too. When our probes didn't find any wildlife, the water was tested and turns out that it's teeming with all sorts of god-awful parasites. This spells a lick of trouble for anyone finding themselves wading through it like we're expecting to—the human body's got a mess of holes in it, and I think it's fairly goddamn obvious why we're having to cover up.

The stretchy, shiny black shorts that Murphy's trying to squeeze his muscular posterior into are completely ludicrous, but they're what Tech came up with to protect against the parasites. They're calling it *prophylactic gear*, but right now it looks like the lot of us is gearing up for an S&M orgy.

It gets my goddamn goat that some soft-skinned, pencil-pushing chair-borne ranger decided on us getting waterproof skivvies under boots 'n' utes rather than outfitting us in proper wet gear. They probably considered it a cost-per-unit solution. Hell, every goddamn year it feels like we get less—next they'll be telling us they can only afford one boot per Marine.

The only upside I see to the stupidly pared-down gear is what it's doing to Murphy's junk. My eyes are drawn again to where his cock is outlined in gorgeous, glossy detail, and I can't help but grin. Murphy notices me watching, and a *V* forms between his brows. You can bet his face is a little pink under all the green and navy war paint, and I feel like laughing, but he's having a time of it as it is.

I pull my dark-green pants up over my own prophylactic gear—nowhere near as flattering on me—and walk over to Murphy. His shorts are pulled up high enough in the front, but at the back, the top of his ass crack is still showing, and the sight of it's got me thinking of other ways to plug his holes.

Get your head in the goddamn game.

I grab a second pair of shorts from the pile, and using a knife and some med tape from the kit on the wall, I quickly make an extension that covers him up. The whole time I'm touching him, Murphy stands still as goddamn stone, and when I glance up, he looks so grateful. You know, I didn't smile half as much before he came around. However, I realize that I might have let the moment go on a little long when I hear the awkward shuffle of boots behind me.

The rest of the squad gets the stink eye when I turn around. I see that Gomez and Singh are fully dressed in their swamp MARPAT cammies, and they're both doing their best to avoid my gaze. Over in the corner, the Ven brothers are involved in some hushed discussion. Then I catch Staff Sergeant Brisbane giving Murphy an appreciative look from across the room, and I curl my lip at him. It takes a moment before he notices me watching him, and when he does, he makes the wise decision to point his ugly goddamn mug at something else. I wish we didn't need him and his men, but we've got a hell of a lot of swamp to cover.

I don't like the way he keeps eyeballing what's mine.

"Why don't y'all get your carcasses to pod bay six instead of grab-assing?" I growl at the room.

Everyone jumps to it—it's all asses and elbows for a second while the men scramble to pick up their rebreathers and packs before heading for the door. Murphy's dressed now, and I turn in time to see him finishing up with his boots. As he gets to his feet, he's got a strange expression on his face. His brows are real low, and it's like he's waiting for something. I notice he's got one hand on his thigh, and his knuckles are white.

"Murph? Something wrong?"

Wide blue eyes flick up to mine. There's a split second of hesitation before he shakes his head and straightens those big shoulders of his. I'm about to tell him to fess up or else he'll have my boot in his ass, when the speakers in the locker room crackle to life.

"Marines, please report to pod bay six." The voice is tinny and robotic and only vaguely female. It repeats itself, then gives the ETA to our destination. We've got a little over ten minutes, and that's not a lot of time considering we still need to get aboard the goddamn drop ship.

I frown at Murphy.

"What is it, son?" Again there's that little pause, but he just shakes his head again.

"Nothin', Sarge," he rumbles. Murph stoops to grab our packs and shoulders his before passing mine over. Our hands meet for a second, and I'm struck with a nearly overwhelming urge to pull him close. I know he can see it clear as fucking day because his eyes widen a smidge. But, since I'm a goddamn imbecile, I just nod my thanks and turn away. If it's not my pecker getting hard, it's something else getting soft. Damn Murphy.

Without another word, I lead us out of the room, thinking about Murphy's weird spot of hesitation again. He's a big boy, and he better goddamn know what he's doing. I can't help it though... I'm worried about what the fuck's bugging him.

The twelve of us are staring out the hell hole of the drop ship—nicknamed the *Stomper* because of its resemblance to some vehicle in a twentieth-century sci-fi movie—and all we can see below us is a rapidly approaching patch of dark, swampy-looking jungle. We're coming down, balls to the fucking wall, about six hundred klicks inland to a spot that's dry enough for a landing but not too far away from our target that we can't make it on foot. It'll take us three days, barring incident, but we're equipped with MREs enough to feed us for five, should we need them.

The trees, big broccoli-looking things, are racing towards us. I'm used to fast drops, probably done about a hundred in my career, but the pucker factor's pretty high, and some of the others look like they're either going to shit their pants or lose their lunches. At least with our prophylactic gear, the stench of shit shouldn't be a problem.

I take a look at Ollie. He's wearing the same gear as the rest of us, except his helmet's probably a good bit older than Murphy. I don't like it. See, I know that's his *lucky* helmet—we've served together a handful of times—and that's got me worried about what he swore up and down and six ways from Sunday would be a low risk op. He sees me watching him and gives me a thumbs-up.

Yeah, I don't like it one fucking bit.

I look over and see that Murph's got his eyes closed. I find that weird and wonder if he's afraid of heights. I don't know him to be afraid of anything, but then again... How well do I know the man? I know every hard curve of his body, every battle scar, every beautiful, fucking needy sound that I can rip out of him. I know he can fieldstrip a weapon in less time than most. I know he can suck cock like he was born to do it. I know he reads a lot of pre-twenty-second-century books... But what else?

He's been sleeping by my side for... oh, I'm guessing half a year or so, and I don't even know what his goddamn favourite food is. I've never asked him. That makes me sad as hell all of a sudden—sadder than I have any goddamn time to feel. Murphy's forehead wrinkles up, and he opens his eyes. He stares at me, the crystal blue of his irises bright, and it hits me then that the colours he sees, they get to him even through his lids. He sees *every goddamn thing* that squeezes this old ticker of mine... all the shit that I can't make myself say.

Jesus fucking Christ, when did I get so fucking maudlin? I shake my head at Murphy and look away, but I can feel his eyes on me.

"Thirty seconds." The Stomper pilot's voice in my ear is so calm it almost sounds bored. Everyone lowers their face shields, snapping them in place. I feel the click a few moments later when our harnesses unlock, and I clutch the handles to either side of me so my head doesn't hit the ceiling. The ground is hurtling up towards us, and without the cushion of the force shield, we'd all be pulverized by the Stomper's sudden stop a moment later. There's a second bump when we make contact with dirt, and the shield winks out as the body of the ship quickly slides towards the ground between the pair of landing legs. We're out the hole the instant we're able to. It's not a far drop, maybe five feet, and everyone lands right. When the comm bead in my ear chirps a warning, we all hit the dirt. Above us, the body of the drop ship springs back up like a snapped rubber, and the Stomper slingshots itself into the air. It's just a speck in one-half less than no time as it races off to the far side of one of the moons to wait for us to complete the mission.

The ground beneath us feels like thick, soggy bread, and now that I'm close enough to see it, there's no actual *dirt* to speak of. It's all moss and roots like stripped wires twisted together. Each step makes a squelching noise, and the air reeks of rotting vegetation. At a nod from me, the men turn off their comms. We're following silent protocol, and that means old-fashioned hand signals or focused-beam communication only.

The second lieutenant is standing with his back to me, staring at the dim 3D topographic map he's holo-casting from his cuff. He spins it around a few times trying to decide which course we should take. The scanners from our probes were only able to give us a fuzzy idea of where we're headed because of the heavy radiation in the upper atmosphere, so there's a bit of guesswork involved.

The mission is simple: find the hidden enemy base and blow it up. Makes sense for the F.I.S.T.S. to be in on this one, considering that's what we accomplished the last time. I glance over at Singh. It's a shame—he used to be a good-looking kid. Even through his face shield, I can see the melted side of his face. Everything works, but cosmetic repair isn't covered. He sees me looking at him and grins wide. Well, at least it didn't kill his enthusiasm.

Murphy's beside me, BFG in hand, and he's turning his head from side to side as he sweeps the jungle around us. I don't know how many others know about his extra sense, but it makes him extraordinarily valuable. He's like a goddamn secret weapon. Sure, he can't "see" through some shielding, but he can see through pretty much everything else. You can't jam his senses like you can a probe's.

Ollie straightens, signals file formation, and we fall in behind him as he starts towards a dense copse of trees. I turn around and walk backwards for a few steps. Pointing at the Ven twins, I motion for them to take the rear and watch our six. The brothers nod and fall back—they were added to my squad because of how brutally effective they are in small-team missions. The only misgivings I have about them are how close they're rumoured to be.

I turn back around. It's really none of my goddamn concern whether they're close as brothers are normally, or if it's something else... except it makes me wonder what the hell would happen if one of them went down. My mind automatically goes to Murphy, and I scowl.

Shit. I wish to hell I could pull my head out of these goddamn dark thoughts about duty and loyalty. It's never been a problem for me before.

MURPHY

The shit we're walking through sucks hard at the soles of my boots with every step, and I can tell it's really starting to wear on the others. We've been walking or wading for about four hours today, and I'm honestly dead on my feet. The past two nights I didn't get much in the way of sleep. The trees around here give off a weird vibe, and my brain's been keeping me awake because of it—that, and the fact that these fucking shorts are really starting to chafe.

Sarge's all tight-jawed over the fact that Ollie—while claiming not to want to usurp Sarge's command in any way—keeps ordering his men about. None of us like it either, but what can we do? We just keep slogging along, hoping to hell that the enemy doesn't know we're here, wishing we could get out of this soup already.

We break through the tree line, and we're headed towards a big lake when the second lieutenant holds up a fist. Everyone comes to a stop. Gomez squelches up to me and slings her thump gun up onto her shoulder. At some point in the last few days, she tore the sleeves off her uniform. The air on this shitty, swampy planet is heavy and dank, and the corded muscles of her arms are shining with sweat and smeared with rotten vegetation. I probably look just as filthy. Sarge and Ollie are in conference over something with the 3D map spinning in the air between them.

"Whattaya make of this, eh, Murph?" Gomez asks me. She's lifted up her face shield, and I can see that her dark curls are plastered across her forehead. I've known her since we were cadets. She's a real Jayne Wayne—completely dependable and something of a virtuoso with an unguided grenade launcher—and one of the few people who knows about my bizarre synaesthesia.

It came out at one point during basic training, and to her credit, she kept it to herself. Gomez talks even less than I do.

"Ollie's confused. Sarge's pissed." At least Ollie is *acting* confused. Something seems off.

Gomez gives a little grunt and nods. She smacks the panel open on her chestplate and pulls out a few protein sticks. I take one when she offers it to me and lift my own visor to stand there chewing it. It's supposed to taste like beef, but it reminds me of sweat.

"Figure this'll end it?" Gomez asks. I figure she means the war, and I shrug. "Ya think we'll get leave when it's over?"

All I can do is shrug again. Leave was abrogated by the military before my career even started, so I've never been on one. It was deemed an unnecessary expense because we're sometimes months getting to our posts. Yeah, because all that time spent travelling through deep space is *just* like being on leave.

The lack of sleep has made me cranky.

As I'm finishing my sweat-flavoured snack, I take a look around. The Ven brothers are standing back-to-back nearby. I don't know much about them to be honest. I think they're identical twins, but it's hard to tell under all that fur. They're the kind who, were they to shave their beards off, would have a hard time deciding where to stop. They don't say much except to each other, but I hear that they're extremely competent and reliable. I certainly get interesting vibes from them, mostly good.

"When we get back, I can see us fixin' to grab a cold one together. What do you say?" The voice in my ear startles me momentarily. My comm bead is turned off, so I turn my head and see that Brisbane is about twenty yards away using an old-fashioned focused-beam comm relay on the sly. It's great for missions like this because you have to be directly in the line of the beam to hear the message—it's very hard to intercept, and it doesn't get picked up on most scanners. Still, he shouldn't be using it for no reason. I shake my head. What is with this guy? The attention is starting to get *real* irritating.

"Oh, c'mon. Just a beer."

I roll my eyes and look away. Sarge is staring at me with a weird look on his face, and what I'm reading from him is that he's angry and sad. I wonder how much the first has to do with the mission, though I know the latter's got to be my doing—I saw it before when we were in the drop ship. What did I do?

Ollie claps Sarge on the shoulder, and Sarge's expression goes into what you could call a glower. Everyone's on edge.

"The base is supposed to be right here," says the second lieutenant. "We can do a sweep of the area. Check to see if there's shielding."

There's a quiet grumble among the men. Could be we've been wasting our time. As everyone gets sorted out into teams and begins to fan out, I look towards the lake. I just saw... something. I frown.

"What is it, Murph?" Sarge clicks his face shield back down.

Yeah, there it is again. Very, very subtle but definitely there—like smoke rising from the smooth surface of the water.

"Maybe it's submerged," I reply.

Ollie looks up in surprise from his map and squints across the lake.

"Well, damn," he says with a chuckle. "That's thinking outside the box, Murphy. I like it." I bend down and fiddle with the straps on the side of my diggies before he has a chance to slap my shoulder too. Yeah, something's not right. I got the feeling that his surprise came from me suggesting the idea, not from the idea itself. I could be wrong though. Ollie takes a few steps towards the lake, scratching his head. The colours coming from him tell me he's annoyed, but that makes no sense... Unless I wasn't supposed to be the one who spots the base. I do a quick three-sixty and see the teams disappearing into the woods. We're the only ones by the water.

I take another long look at the lake. There's something down there all right. The repetitiveness to the slight shimmer reminds me of a ship's engines—means there's machinery. I can't catch anything else though.

"How the fuck do we get to it?" asks Sarge.

I want to tell him that I suspect Ollie knows far more than he's letting on, but how? I straighten and shift in place before the ground swallows any more of my boot. Thankfully, the leg's behaving itself at the moment.

Ollie swipes at his map and then spins it on a different axis before punching a few things into his cuff.

"Take into account that it's water..." he mutters, stroking his little moustache. "Uh huh. Add this... hm... figure it's what"—he looks over at me and Sarge—"three hundred metres across?"

"Give or take."

"Ok, now we're talking!" Ollie straightens the holo out. "Looks like it's not that deep." He's superimposed the map with something else, and suddenly it's showing us a cross-section of the lake. That was way too fucking easy... I glance up and notice that Ollie's watching me. The smile on his face is friendly, but the colours around him are suspicion and determination. I smooth the frown off my face and make my expression bland.

"Uh... Yup," I say and scratch my nose a bit. "Uh... We gonna swim?" I see that my numbskull routine mollifies him slightly, and he nods.

"Looks like!" says Ollie, seeming full of good cheer. Then he glances down. "You sure you can handle the swim, Murphy?"

"Y'sir." I'm a decent swimmer.

"How's the ol' leg?"

I frown. *My leg?*

"Sir?"

"It's feeling ok? All this water not causing any problems?"

I look down at my right leg. My cammies are soaked through and covered in dark green slime. What the fuck does he know about my leg?

"Leg's fine, sir." I can barely hear myself think above the warning bells going off in my skull. Ollie just gives me an odd look before nodding.

"If Murph says he's fine, he's fine." I can see Sarge has caught a whiff of my suspicion. "But before we dive in, I'd like to wait until the teams report back to—"

"Nonsense," says Ollie, cheerfully cutting him off. "They're searching trees. We're searching water. Only difference is we're going to get wetter than they are. Just a little recon, and we'll regroup. We're only checking to see if your boy Murphy is right about the base."

Before I have a chance to pull Sarge to the side, Ollie's slipping the rebreather over his head and motioning for us to do the same.

"Let's go," he says, snapping the hoses into the intakes in the face shield. "Time's a-wasting!"

Sarge and I share a glance behind Ollie's back as he wades into the water. I know that we're thinking the same thing:

What the fuck is going on?

I'm light-headed, and colours are spinning in my vision as I try to concentrate on breathing. We're in the submerged base, being power blasted with some chemical that I hope is meant to kill the parasites, but I'm *this* close to passing out. I made the relatively short swim underwater wearing the rebreather, but these things aren't made for a guy my size. It makes barely enough oxygen for me to survive, and that's made worse by the fact that I had to work twice as hard to swim—feels like my leg is starting to glitch again.

Finally the lights blink out, and the airlock hatch opens with a long *hiss*. I rip the mask off my face and take in a few huge gulps of air. I'm going to have one hell of a headache in a minute, but right now I'm worried about the fact that we've just let ourselves in like we own the place.

Ollie slips off his own mask, and Sarge looks around, confusion all over his face. I can see why—this isn't an enemy base. I'm sure that if I opened any of the wall panels, I'd see the *ESAD Defence Corp.* logo etched in the metal.

This is one of ours.

"What in Christ's name is going on?" growls Sarge. The second lieutenant looks at him for a long moment and decides to drop the pretence.

"I can explain all of this, Wilkes," he says.

I take a step towards Sarge. At least that was my intent. Instead, I put my foot forward and promptly collapse.

"Great. *Now* it happens." Ollie sounds exasperated.

My leg is completely dead. I can't move it at all, and I'm suddenly pretty fucking sure Ollie knows why. I'm reacting rather than thinking when I point my BFG at him. There's water pouring out of it, but it'll fire regardless. It's not just about my leg—I have to keep Sarge safe.

"Whoa there, big fella," Ollie says and lifts his hands. "Take it easy." His eyes bug when he feels the barrel of Sarge's pistol against his temple. Sarge isn't thinking straight either if he's pissed enough to put a gun to his superior officer's head.

"Talk."

"Put down your weapons."

"What the hell is this, Ollie?"

"Wilkes, I'm on your side. Just put down the pistol and call your boy off so we can all have a nice chit-chat."

At that moment, the door down the hallway slides open, and I quickly turn my charge rifle on the man who emerges. When he freezes in place, I see that he's dressed in the same uniform any tech would wear aboard our starcruisers. I can even see the logo embroidered on the front.

Ollie uses the distraction to his advantage and knocks the gun out of Sarge's hand. They grapple on the deck while I keep my weapon trained on the man. My brain is spinning through possibilities, but without my leg, there's a limit to what I can do, and no amount of thinking will get it to budge.

Shit.

The little fucker in the tech uniform doesn't look like he'll pull a weapon—I can see he's scared shitless.

I take a gamble and turn the BFG on the two men, slam the toggle back, and let loose with a bolt that hits Ollie square in the ass. It takes a bit of a struggle before Sarge is able to push the second lieutenant off, and I glance back at the tech just in time to see the blue pulse belch out of the weapon he's holding. The charge hits me full in the chest.

Sarge

As Murphy slumps to the deck, I let out a yell and grab for my pistol. The man with the pulse gun dives behind what looks like a bank of computers before I have a chance to let off a goddamn shot. I'm a sitting duck, so I slide over closer to the airlock door for cover.

One look at Murph reassures me. Seems like the shielding on his chestplate took the brunt of the charge—there isn't much of the usual charred-meat smell—but he's out cold. Beside me on the ground, Ollie lets out a moan. Murphy only hit him with a stun bolt, so he's coming out of it too fucking quickly. I want to tie the treasonous shitheel up, but I don't have the goddamn time. He rubs his face and blinks, grimacing at the pistol I've got pointed between his eyes.

"We're under fire," I snarl at him. I'm madder than a bag of cats at being caught out like this. "You're gonna help me drag Murphy, and so help me god, if you do so much as twitch, I'm going to *end* you."

"Under... fire?" The stun seems to have shaken him. He looks confused. "Oh goddamnit! The base was supposed to be clear." He swears under his breath and rubs his face. Then, before I can stop him, Ollie shouts.

"Stand down! Do you hear me? Stand down! We're friendlies." I'm incredulous as all hell when Ollie winks at me. "We're only here to collect the latest research files. Clearance code zero whiskey tango foxtrot niner."

There's a rustle, and a moment later, the technician emerges slowly from behind his cover. He's gotta be nineteen... twenty, tops.

Quick as a whip, Ollie grabs the pistol from my hand and sends a charge through the kid's throat. He's dead before he even hits the deck. I watch as a little smoke rises from the body.

Ollie calmly pops the charge pack out of my pistol, drops it on the ground, and kicks it away. It slides under what looks like an old-fashioned filing cabinet.

"Sorry about that," he says. "Can't have you going off half-cocked, not knowing what you're getting into." He glances over at Murphy. "Is he...?"

"Unconscious." I can see the rise and fall of Murphy's chest. As much as I want to go over and make sure he's all right, I have to get to the goddamn bottom of this.

"I really am sorry," he says again. "I was told that the base was going to be completely empty. Someone screwed up." Ollie shakes his head, then looks down at his cuff. "I don't see any other life signs. We should be good." It's as if he didn't just kill a kid in cold blood.

"What the hell is going on?" This is a goddamn nightmare.

Ollie lets out a long sigh and then looks up at the ceiling tiles like he's searching for answers.

"This stays between you and me, Wilkes. Top secret. You say anything, you'll be prosecuted to the highest extent of the law." He fixes me all steely-eyed. I guess I don't have a goddamn choice, so I nod.

"This wasn't supposed to happen. Murphy's leg was supposed to short out before we got to the lake. We were supposed t—"

"Murphy's leg? What the hell did you do to it?" I remember the way Murphy's knuckles were turning white as he clutched at it.

"Me? Nothing. Just a neural block set up to make it fail—he should have been feeling it for weeks now, bit by bit and getting worse the closer we got. I don't get why it didn't work. Cheap electronics? Or..." Ollie sees the look on my face and frowns. "Ok, long story short: he collapses, and you stay with him and keep a few men with you. The rest of us 'discover' the lake, then Brisbane takes part of the squad to search the woods, and I take a couple of jarheads to do the swim. I grab the latest research, set the base to self-destruct, it blows up and—Bob's your uncle—we're all heroes and no one's the wiser about the nature of this facility." Ollie chuckles. "But, well... even the best laid plans..."

"Explain *that*," I growl, pointing to the dead tech in the *ESAD Defence Corp.* jumpsuit. "And all *this*. What the good goddamn *is* 'the nature of this facility'?"

"It's a branch of R&D. Mostly genetics. Top secret stuff." He goddamn waves it off like it's nothing and then sighs again. "Wilkes, it's our bottom line. It's the third quarter in a row where we're not meeting our forecasted growth. We *have* to show few solid victories to our backers or else we're going to face more cuts. So, instead of going after an enemy base with only a forty percent mission success rate, we can blow up one of our own with a *one hundred percent* mission success rate. Plus, when we discover 'alien' research that we can use to our advantage? Well, I'm sure that'll bring more investors to the table."

"This is about *money*?" The shock on my face has got to be spectacular because he gives another one of those annoying little white-toothed chuckles and shakes his head.

"It's always been about money. Believe me, after today we'll see a rise in projected capital, guaranteed, and the war stays profitable. Everyone wins! And, I'll personally make sure that your little squad gets top-of-the-line from now on."

All those lives lost. All that waste. Always told that we're ill equipped because we don't have the money. Projected capital? What, the corporation is making plenty of money, but not as much *more* money as they would like? I think about the corporate shareholders, lining their pockets with what could have spared so many lives. What about Murphy, lying in my lap, bleeding out with his leg torn off? What if we had been properly outfitted for the mission? I think I let out a groan.

"Oh, c'mon, Wilkes. Like I said, you weren't supposed to see this. You're valuable, and you know what? So is your boyfriend. I personally calculated the benefit of keeping you off to the side during this mission. I was keeping you *safe*.

Boyfriend? It startles me for half a beat, but I push it aside.

"Why the fuck have me on the mission at all then?" I can't keep the anger out of my voice.

"Like I said. You're valuable. Just having you on this mission increased the profitability margin by three points."

My mind is still reeling with the fact that *safe* is only safe when it's cost-efficient. Then I remember something he said.

"And the men you were planning on bringing with you here? What was the plan when they realized you were blowing up our own base? And what about that kid? *Christ*, did you have to kill the kid?"

"*Less* valuable... Acceptable loss—"

I have him up against the bulkhead, my forearm jammed across his throat, in an instant.

"Those are *men*," I yell at him. "Not goddamn numbers. Not resources. Not fucking dollar signs. Those are human fucking beings!" I'm beyond furious when I slam my fist into his face, and I'm gratified somewhat when feel cartilage crack against my knuckles. Ollie's shout of pain just makes me punch him harder. Then, for good measure, I grab him by the collar to start bashing his head on the wall. The man's stick-thin, no match for me. I'm seeing red... the blood of all those men who died in duty because they didn't have a big enough dollar sign attached to them.

"Sarge." Murphy's voice is hoarse and quiet, but the sound of it cuts straight through my anger and immediately shakes me out of it. I drop the second lieutenant and fall to my knees in front of my boy. He looks a little pale under the camouflage paint, and his breath sounds laboured.

"Are you ok?" I clasp the hand he holds out to me, and he lets out a pained grunt as I help him to sit up.

"Yeah. Think so." He winces as I start undoing the buckles on his chestplate. "Better'n him." Murphy pushes my hand away and continues to gingerly work on the straps himself. I look over my shoulder to where Ollie's lying on his side with his face smashed in.

"He can go to hell."

"Then you're no different. Ouch *fuck*." I turn back to Murphy.

He's opened his scorched shirt and is staring down at his bare chest where there's a clear outline of the armour burned into his skin. "Well, that's different," he mutters. Then he looks up at me, his blue eyes sober.

"Sarge, he's a man. Said it yourself."

Goddamn it. I scrub at my face tiredly and then nod.

You know, people who think they've got the dynamic between me and Murph pegged... Well, they don't know they got it backwards.

Murphy unclips his service pistol from his hip to hand it to me, just in case we're not actually alone, and I go on the search for a med unit so I can make sure Second Lieutenant Oliver Grunwalt doesn't become just another acceptable loss.

Murphy

I'm lying on my side in the small med bay, my head on Sarge's thigh, and he's sorta just stroking the back of my neck. Since none of the cots are wide enough to hold the both of us, Sarge salvaged a few thin mattresses and arranged them on the floor up against a wall. With my leg the way it is and Ollie in tow, there's no way we can make the swim back to the surface right now. But, there are plenty of supplies in the research facility, so we're in no danger of starving any time soon. Sarge has turned his comm back on, seeing as there aren't actually any of the enemy on this planet, and has it set to relay our coordinates every fifteen minutes or so. The squads above will either eventually turn on comms to try to make contact or just figure out themselves where we are and come get us—it's only a matter of time. Meanwhile, we wait.

Across the room, Ollie's hooked up to a unit that's busy repairing his brain damage. Since he's an officer, cosmetic repairs fall under budget, so he's even getting his nose fixed. Lucky guy.

I heard everything Ollie said... All that crap about money, and bottom lines, and acceptable losses. It's shitty, but he's just obeying orders from on high. Just like me. Just like Sarge. Doesn't mean I'm not pissed off about it, but letting the man die isn't going to change anything. I'm glad I got through to Sarge.

"How's your leg?"

I try to move it again with no result.

"Still dead."

"Damn."

I smile. The one good thing that comes out of this is that I know there's nothing wrong with me. My leg was sabotaged... It had nothing to do with brain damage from the neural relays.

Neural relays...

I lift my head and squint at the shelves nearby. There are boxes of bandages, refill cartridges for the sequencers, blister packs of something blue...

"What is it?" asks Sarge.

I'm only mildly burned and bruised from the charge blast, but holding my head up begins to hurt my chest, so I push myself to sitting. I spot a stack of the familiar gunmetal-grey cases that the relays come in, and I point to them.

"Maybe with a little more brainpower we can reboot my leg."

Ollie said it was a neural block. I'm thinking it's just a chip set up to interrupt my control of the leg. Might not be strong enough to withstand the added juice Sarge could provide. If that's the case, we might be able to fry it and get my leg working again. Who knows? It's worth a shot.

Sarge gets to his feet and grabs one of the cases. Then he rifles through a plexi-resin box on the next shelf. When he comes back to sit next to me, I see he's found some hubba. I wave it off and take the relays from him.

"Not hurt that bad."

"Bullshit. You're hurt enough, son. And if I'm gonna be in your head, you can be damn sure I don't want to feel it," says Sarge with a smirk. I let him stick me with the single-dose shot and almost instantly I get this hazy numb feeling that dampens the pain in my chest.

"Better?"

I let out a small grunt and nod. Yeah, it feels nice. I've got the relays out and see that they're brand new, never been used before. I peel off the clear protectors, and I stick one on my temple and the other on Sarge's. It only takes a few seconds before I feel the familiar flow of energy between us. Because of the painkiller in my system, the connection is a little different this time. Good different. I grin as I watch the colours shift around us, pulsing and growing as Sarge relays what I'm feeling back to me. It's pretty cool.

"Murphy?" says Sarge, and I try to focus on his face. "You look stoned."

"Yup." I reach out for him and pull him towards me. I *need* to kiss him. Our mouths meet, sorta clumsy because of the angle. I want to... fuck... I don't even know. I want to show him just how much I need him.

I guess I go a little overboard because Sarge pushes me away, frowning.

"Jesus, Andrew." He never calls me that. It *does* something to me... And shit, now I can't figure out what Sarge's feeling because everything is so intense. Did he give me too much hubba? Maybe it's just the lack of sleep... or maybe I'm imagining things because everything seems fine again when Sarge lifts his hand to touch my lips. I open obediently so that he can slide two fingers into my mouth, and I suck on them gently, watching the pleasure come off him in subtle waves... but there's sadness there too. It's the same as before. He looks confused when I pull away from him.

"Why're you sad?" I ask.

Sarge's lips press tight, and the muscles in his jaw move. I reach up to touch the rough grey stubble on his chin, but he takes my hand in his instead. When he finally speaks, his voice is quiet. His thumb strokes my palm.

"Son... Do I..." He looks like he's struggling with the words, and his voice goes rough. "Do I make you *happy*?"

I blink, startled. I want to laugh, but Sarge might take that the wrong way.

"Y'sir." When I try to pull his hand back to my mouth, he stops me.

"I'm serious."

"So'm I," I rumble. Happy? Hell, I've never been happier or felt more at peace than the months I've spent at Sarge's side.

"I treat you all right?" he asks. His brown eyes are wide. I feel a surge of something naked and raw come from him. My heart feels like it's trying to batter its way out of my chest. Where is this all coming from? Why this doubt?

"Course, Sarge. Always."

"So you wouldn't rather be with someone else? Someone

closer to your own age, like Brisbane?"

The look of disgust on my face makes him laugh, breaking up the tension for a second.

"Ok. Not Brisbane," he says with a nod. "No one else?"

"N'sir."

He grabs my jaw with the other hand and just stares hard at me for a sec.

"I just... Shit, son—I just want to make sure *this* is really what you want."

Thinking back to the day I promised him I'd always obey, I smile. I remember how overwhelmed with relief I'd been over finally having found real freedom.

I nod and Sarge lets go of my face, still searching my eyes for something.

I duck forward and brush my lips up the line of his jaw, soft and slow, my warm breath fanning back to me.

"*Yours.*" I murmur it against his skin then press a kiss to the sensitive spot beneath his ear. I hear a little grumbly noise from him, and I sit back with a sheepish smile. His brows are pinched over his nose, and he looks like he's in severe pain as a wild storm of colours swirls around us.

Finally he lets out a shaky breath and chuckles low.

"Goddamn it, Murphy." He clutches the back of my head and pulls me forward so our foreheads meet for a moment. I close my eyes and just let everything wash over me. Yeah... This is *exactly* where I belong.

Sarge releases me and nudges me backwards on the mattress without a word. As I move, I realize that my leg is working again... but I don't say anything. Now's not the time. All I'm wearing is a pair of too-short scrub pants—scavenged from a locker because I had to get out of those fucking shorts—and his hand feels good through the thin cotton when he slides it over my cock. I let out a slow breath and shift, giving into the gentleness.

Just as I'm wishing for real contact, Sarge grins and tugs the waistband of the pants down. He holds his hand out to my face.

"Spit."

I lift my head and spit obediently into his palm. He adds some of his own and then wraps his hand around my cock and starts to jerk me off slowly. It feels so good, but saliva dries up quick.

"Hang on." Sarge gets off the makeshift bed and goes digging through the cupboards and drawers until he finds something that makes him smile. He snags a pillow on his way back to me and helps me stuff it under my ass after dragging the scrubs all the way off. Then he begins to pour the surgical lubricant he found all over my dick. The gel is cold, but he quickly begins to work my cock, hand over slippery hand, and soon has me straining up and moaning in a way that would normally embarrass me.

"You're going to tell me when to stop," says Sarge.

"Aye'sir." Sarge chuckles to himself when my voice breaks a little. My balls are tight, and I can feel the lube sliding down between my cheeks as Sarge strokes me. My cockhead rubs through the opening of his thumb and finger once more, and I'm almost beside myself. I clench my teeth.

"Stop."

Instantly, Sarge lets go. For a second I think it's too late, but my cock just bobs up from my stomach once and then lies back down obediently.

"Now. You're going to count to fifty then ask me to do it again."

Breathing hard, I nod. Fifty seconds pass and I'm in control again, but I frown thinking about what he said. Ask him to touch me again? How? Hell, I'm no good with words. In fact, just thinking about it makes my face hot. I open my mouth, but nothing comes out. Sarge just watches me, amused and aroused.

"Please..."—I let out a few short breaths—"Again?"

"Good boy. Now, same drill: you tell me to stop, count to fifty, and ask me again. This time I want you to tell me *exactly* what it is you want me doing to you."

I blink at him and then nod. I'm so turned on that it only takes a dozen or so strokes before I'm teetering on the edge. I manage to break out a "Stop!" before I cum in his hand. Fifty seconds later, I'm red-faced again, wondering how specific he wanted me to be.

"Please... Want you to touch me..." I try hesitantly. Just saying those words makes me squirm.

Sarge's laugh is low and almost evil-sounding. "Son, you're gonna have to do better than that."

Argh.

"Please uh..." *Fuck.* "Please rub my dick..." Shit, it's one thing to repeat after him, completely another to come up with the words on my own.

He grins and continues to jerk me off.

I have no idea how long it's been going on. More lube, more stroking... Stop... Ask please... Repeat. All I know is that I can barely form a thought in my head, the mattress beneath me is soaked in sweat, and I'm going insane. Still Sarge keeps working on my cock, but now he's got two fingers up inside me, rubbing at my prostate. I'm covered in lube and precum and probably some tears. Shit, I can't even articulate what I want anymore so I just keep saying *stop* and *please, stop* and *please.* I'm starting to hate the number fifty.

I finish my count, and I let out a strangled sound as his palm rubs the weeping head of my cock. He barely has to touch me before I need him to stop.

This time, Sarge is jerking his own dick while I count. When I say *please,* he doesn't take me in hand again. No, he shifts in place and presses the head of his cock against my pucker. I shut my eyes, breathing quickly as he forces me open and slides himself deep.

"I know you don't love this," he says quietly as he starts to fuck me with slow thrusts. "But, I love fucking your tight hole. I fucking love it."

Contrary to what he just said, I'm actually loving it too right now—all this edging has me as greedy for it as he is, and oh, he knows it. I grab him around the hips and pull him into me hard. Sarge lets out a little huff of breath and moves back, purposefully staying shallow so I'll force him into me deep again.

"Oh Christ," he gasps. "That's it. Just like that. Balls-deep in your ass... That's where my dick belongs, doesn't it, son? That's my good boy." The way his cock is curved means that he's hitting my prostate with every languid thrust, and I'm starting to make these broken little whimpers because I am getting really close... and it's hard as hell to hold back... and I've got my heels pushing into his lower back...

"Please..."

Sarge lets out a grunt and starts thrusting into me faster. I swear he's trying to fuck the cum right out of me, but then he wraps his hand around my dick, and it's all over for me. The surge that comes out of my cock forces a yell out of me as my ass pulses and throbs over the thick shaft buried inside me. Sarge's got his head down, rutting hard, growling low, and then he pulls out, fist moving fast over his dick.

"Open your mouth."

I do him one better and quickly swivel round, up on my hands and knees in front of him, mouth wide, tongue out, eyes up to his. He lets out a deep groan, and I make a needy sound of my own just as a hot stream of cum lands on my tongue. He milks his cock, eyes narrow and mouth open in a breathy pant as he empties his balls and coats my lips and the back of my throat.

Sarge chuckles softly and puts a hand on my head as he tries to catch his breath. Then he gently pushes me away so that I'm once again on my back. He swipes at my chest with the balled-up pants, clearing away the worst of what hasn't made it to the mattress already, then collapses next to me with a long, pleased sigh. I turn over on my side and nuzzle into his neck sleepily— Sarge rewards me with a soft, stroking touch down my back. I could sleep for a week, I'm so exhausted.

"Mine..." He says it so quietly I barely hear him.

"Mm." I'm glad we're in complete agreement.

SARGE

Less than twenty-four hours after we stepped foot in the underwater base, we're contacted by the team on land. It was Brisbane that decided to check the comms. He's an asshole, but we've got him to thank for our imminent rescue. He's put in a request for a small shuttlecraft to come get us—even though Murphy's leg is working again, it's not at 100 percent, and I'd hate for it to cut out while we're taking the swim.

Then there's the second lieutenant to think about. Ollie's awake finally and damn grateful I didn't kill him, but he's in no shape to do any swimming at the moment.

Command is probably sitting up there, pacing back and forth, wearing the shine off the deck and wondering what in the hell they're going to do. Why? Well, I just sent them a wave saying that I have in my possession years of research that they were going to pass off as "alien". It's all illegal stuff—mostly genetic manipulation that's been outlawed since the gene wars triggered one of the biggest periods of intolerance the human race has ever faced: the "Fanatical Forties". Though that was before my time, the repercussions are still felt to this goddamn day... Jesus, if the federated governments knew that the military corporation was conducting those sorts of experiments? Heads would fucking roll. Problem is, I'm not sure whether it would be the right ones.

I still haven't decided what I'm going to do with the information, but in the meantime, I've uploaded it to a number of safe places and made sure that if anything happens to me, it finds its way to the right people.

In return for me sitting on the research for now, I'm thinking of asking for my own ship. Nothing huge. Maybe a Thanatos class frigate... just something big enough for my little squad. We're a crack team—imagine what we could accomplish if we weren't so shackled to the bureaucracy?

I've lost my faith, you might say. I gave my life... my *whole fucking life* to this uniform. I sacrificed my goddamn youth, my family, my health, and my humanity to duty. Yeah, I did my duty, and I did it well. And what did I get in return? Bullshit. *Acceptable fucking losses.* A great big *fuck-you.*

My eyes are open to it now. I think I've known what was happening for a long goddamn time but was too blinded and entombed by my career to notice. Then, while I was doing my goddamn duty, my life passed me by. You know how I feel? I feel *robbed.*

I hear a soft noise and I look up. Murphy's wide blue eyes are like a salve, cooling the burns that blister up my insides. The rage calms, and when he tilts his head a little to ask me if I'm all right, I smile and nod.

Now's not the right time to be bringing information to light that will sure as shit trigger a restructuring. Believe me, I'd be happier than all hell if we went back to the olden days when it was the Space Marine *Corps*, not *Corporation*. But, despite all the bullshit about poorly allocated resources, fat cat investors, and downright treasonous doings, the truth of the matter is that there's still a goddamn war going on. A war to be *won*, dammit, profitable or not. There are good men out there that need our help, and we're going to give it to them.

Yeah... I'll be fine. I'll be just fine, as long as I have Murphy by my side. I guess I was wrong about it being too late for an old bastard like me.

I watch Murphy finish up with the straps to the gurney that Ollie is strapped to and pile the second lieutenant's things at the foot of it. His brow creases, and his eyes get distant for a moment, listening to the shuttle pilot's voice in his ear.

"Roger that," he says, his voice just a deep rumble in that huge chest. "We'll be at the airlock in five. Yeah, *tango*." He sees me watching him, and he smiles that half-shy smile that dimples his cheek only on one side. Then Murphy turns to push the gurney through the hatch with a slight limp in his normally smooth gait.

Gorgeous and gifted with as much brains as brawn... and unwaveringly and completely mine. I grit my teeth and blink hard. There must be dust in my eye.

He rescued me, my boy. From myself, mostly. And, you can bet your ass that from now until forever, I'm going to make every single goddamn second count.

"Hey, Murphy," I call out.

"Yeah, Sarge?"

"Tell me about your favourite food, son..."

The Missing Reel

BEY DECKARD

I originally left this very short scene out when I wrote Sarge because I wanted the nature of their relationship to be somewhat ambiguous.

I'm glad I get to share it with you now.
Enjoy!

MURPHY

I'm alone in the harsh light of the passageway, staring at the name on the door: Sgt. Reginald Wilkes. Behind me, the window shows a darkened wasteland, only relieved of the pure pitch of night by the twin yellow moons in orbit. In less than an hour, the massive red sun will bake this side of the planet, but for the moment, the barrack's A/C units seem to be working fine—a rarity these days—and the air is cool enough that I'm not overheating in my service uniform.

I take a few deep breaths. I can't remember the last time I was so nervous. I swear clearing fucking reaver caves has nothing on this.

Calm yourself, keep it together... and don't get your hopes up, stupid.

I sigh. The last is almost impossible. Why else would he have called for me? Finally, I rap quickly on the gunmetal-grey resin, right above the glossy letters.

"Come on in!" is the response from the other side, so I tug hard on the khaki button-up shirt to straighten it and take my garrison cap off to tuck it under my belt. Feeling like my heart's stuck up against my Adam's apple, I open the door and take a step in.

Sarge is sitting in an old rolling chair that's seen better days. He's got a slight frown on his face, but I can see that he's happy to see me, and *fuck* if that doesn't just send my pulse racing some more. This is the first time I've seen him since he got his eye fixed, and though it's only been a week, I've been sitting on pins and needles every day hoping to hear from him.

I stand at attention, and he gets to his feet, his dark-brown eyes serious as he looks up at me. Quickly averting my gaze, I focus on the wall behind him, not wanting him to see how nervous I am. Sarge promised to show me "what good boys get" and... if that's why I'm here...

Fuck, I hope that's why I'm here.

"Private First Class Andrew Murphy," he says gruffly in greeting.

"Asked for me, sir?" I reply, relieved at how composed I sound.

Sarge steps around me and shuts the door. When I hear the lock turn with a quiet *click*, I let out a small huff of breath and try to relax, but I'm giddy beyond belief. A few seconds pass where I can feel his eyes moving over me, and the small hairs on the back of my neck stand up as my skin prickles from scalp to rib cage from the scrutiny.

The air around me is bathed in the rich hues of desire.

I feel Sarge's body heat through my clothes as he walks past me to stand a few paces away. Though he isn't a short man—just over six feet according to his sheet—I still manage to dwarf him. However, it doesn't seem to bother him in the least.

"Take off your clothes." It's spoken as a command. Impersonal.

Startled, I blink and focus on him. He's got a wrinkle between his brows, waiting for me to obey, and I have to admit that I wasn't expecting him to just jump straight into *this*. Flustered and suddenly too hot, I start to undo the buttons of my shirt. I glance at him when I get to the end of the row, and he nods at me to continue. With a yank, my shirt comes out of my trousers. I do away quickly with the white undershirt and then pause, hands at my belt, when I hear Sarge's long exhale.

I look up from what I'm doing and see that his expression has gone sorta vague. Sarge is handsome in that strong-jawed, hawk-nosed, grizzled kind of way. His face is weathered from age with deep creases next to his mouth and across his forehead—only the skin around his new eye is smooth—but nothing about him is *soft*. Sarge is famous for being hard as fucking nails, so the look on his face is something I never dreamed of seeing.

He looks *awed*.

I feel my cheeks burn as I undo my pants, but before I pull them down, I crouch to undo my boots. It affords me a moment of respite to try to still my shaking hands. In all, it probably takes less than a minute before I'm standing naked in front of my commanding officer.

I shyly turn my eyes to him and watch as he comes closer.

Sarge lifts a hand to run it slowly over my chest. The contact pulls an involuntary sound out of me, and I shut my eyes for a second, wondering if he can feel how fast my heart is beating right now.

His fingers find my nipple, and he plays with it, brushing the pad of his thumb over the sensitive, stiffening flesh. Then he pinches—soft at first and then hard enough that I wince and let out a small grunt. Sarge chuckles. His hand moves further down, and his fingers slide along the long scar I got from being near-gutted by a reaver.

All the while, I'm trying to gauge whether I should be looking at him as he inspects me. Part of me thinks I should be keeping my gaze up, but I'm almost mesmerized by the way his eyes crease in appreciation as he strokes over the ridges of my obliques and then back across and down to test the hardness of my abs.

When his fingers finish their trip down the line of my pelvis, he looks at me straight in the eye. There is absolutely no hiding the fact that I am incredibly aroused, as evidenced by the turgid thickness of the root his fingers encircle, and I clench my jaw as he squeezes my cock with a warm, dry hand.

"That *is* a goddamn rocket launcher," he says with a grin. His other hand slides over my hip to grab my backside hard. "Spread your legs, son." He gives my ass a firm, stinging slap.

I shift my legs apart while trying to hide the fact that I'm having a hard time breathing. I haven't been touched in a good long while, and I don't want to seem overly eager, but the way my dick keeps throbbing in Sarge's grasp probably has him clued into *exactly* how much I want this.

"You cleaned yourself?"

My face feels like it's on fire. "Y'sir."

Sarge chuckles again and slides his fingers between my ass cheeks to begin stroking at my hole gently. The sound that comes out of me borders on a whimper, and I have to look away. There's being naked, and then there's being made to *feel* naked—what Sarge is doing has me completely stripped bare, and I am hovering between elation and tearful embarrassment.

"Healthy?" It takes me a sec to recognize that he's asked me a question, and I swallow.

"Y'sir."

"You're up to date with all your shots?" He shifts his hand away from stroking my asshole so he can cup my balls from behind, squeezing and pulling on them gently.

"Y'sir."

"Do you know why you're here, son?"

My eyes dart to his.

"N'sir."

"Well, that's a goddamn lie," he says, shaking his head. The hand around my balls tightens, and I let out a nervous breath. "You sure as hell know why you're here."

"Y'sir," I manage. I'm sweating despite it being cool in the room. His hand slowly runs along my shaft, and then he rubs his palm against the head of it. The feeling is so intense that I hiss out a breath between my teeth.

"And why's that?"

The words stall in my throat for a second as his hand makes a second pass over my cockhead, slicker this time.

"Y'said... good boys... uh, get—" I mumble but choke to a stop when he starts playing at my hole again. I've never been fondled so... casually before. I feel utterly exposed.

"And are you a good boy, Murphy?"

Oh, yes. Oh, *fuck* yes, am I a good boy. There's nothing in the world I want to do right now other than show him *exactly* how good I can be, but I just nod quickly instead, not trusting myself to words.

"Oh? You are?" Sarge's hand stops caressing my dick, and the fingers ghosting my hole drop away. Suddenly, I wonder if I should have said "no". I look at him, my eyes pleading. I *need* this—I don't want to fuck this up.

His brows pinch over his nose as he stares at me. Lust is coming off him in waves, but there's something else there too that I didn't expect: apprehension.

"Let's get one thing straight. You're here, son, because I want to fuck that gorgeous ass of yours. I want to gag you on my cock and cum all over your goddamn face. I want you licking my boots and obeying my every goddamn word. I want to *own* this." He gives my dick a hard squeeze, and I only barely stifle my needy sound by turning it into a soft grunt. "Do you understand me, Marine? I want a warm hole that I can shove my dick into without worrying about whether you want it or not."

Despite his brusque tone, my eyes go wide with the realization that he's proposing something more than just today.

"Y'sir!" This time I can't keep the eagerness out of my voice, and Sarge looks a little startled. He lets go of my dick and takes a step back, frowning at me. I know that, though he's being honest with me, he's also trying to scare me off.

Thing is, I don't scare easily, especially when I know exactly what I want.

I drop down to my knees, bowing my head, and there's a long pause as Sarge just stands there. In stillness, I patiently wait for him to surrender to me and trust that *this* is where I belong.

Finally, he speaks up.

"I don't like complicated rules, son, and I don't wanna have to discuss every goddamn thing with you. I'm a simple man, and I like to keep it that way," he says quietly. His hand cups my chin, and he coaxes my head up. Sarge searches my eyes for something, and I just breathe slowly, watching him. My own emotions are getting in the way of things. I can't tell what he's thinking, so I say the only word that comes to mind:

"*Please.*"

Sarge's mouth twitches to the side, and he swallows. He

strokes my cheek with a thumb before replying.

"Well... Do you have a word, son? One you can use when I get too rough with you?" he asks all gentle.

When, not *if*.

I trust him with my life—both on the battlefield and off. How to make him understand that having a fail-safe degrades that trust? I barely understand it myself, this burning need to put myself entirely into the hands of another, but it's there... and it's like nothing else.

I shake my head.

Sarge's eyebrows hitch up.

"You got that much trust in me?"

One tight nod from me makes his expression go vague again. This time I catch a glimpse of something through the tiny break in his armour: longing.

I turn my head so that I can rub my lips against his palm.

Sarge sighs and then slides his hand up the side of my face to rest it on top of my head. I close my eyes. Nearly a full minute passes before he takes a step back, and I hear the clink of his belt buckle. I look up at him as he pulls a thick, uncut cock out of his pants.

"You better learn to love the taste of my cum, son," he says, stroking himself with a grim expression, "or else this is gonna be a waste of my goddamn time."

I have to work to keep the smile off my face.

"Aye'sir."

OTHER BOOKS BY BEY DECKARD

For an up-to-date list of titles, visit:
https://beydeckard.com/blog/buy-my-books/

Max, the Series
Max
Max, the Sequel

Baal's Heart Series
Caged: Love and Treachery on the High Seas
Sacrificed: Heart Beyond the Spires
Fated: Blood and Redemption
Careened: Winter Solstice in Madierus

F.I.S.T.S
Sarge
Murphy
F.I.S.T.S. Handbook For Individual Survival in Hostile Environments

The Actor's Circle
The Complications of T
The Last Nights of The Frangipani Hotel

The Stonewatchers
Kestrel's Talon

Standalone Books
Toxic AF
Uncle Zach
Better the Devil You Know
Exposed
Beauty and His Beast
The Blacksmith's Apprentice

ABOUT THE AUTHOR
Artist, Writer, Dog Lover

Bey Deckard is the author of a number of novels including the *Baal's Heart books*, *Max*, *Beauty and His Beast*, and *Better the Devil You Know*.

Bey lives in Montréal, Canada where he spends most of his time writing, doing graphic work, painting portraits, speaking French, cooking tasty vegetarian eats, or watching more movies than is good for him. If you're the curious type, www.beydeckard.com is where you'll find art and free stories by Bey as well as information on his published works.

bey.deckard@gmail.com

Look for Deckard's Diablerie on Facebook

www.ingramcontent.com/pod-product-compliance
Lightning Source LLC
Chambersburg PA
CBHW061248170626
46809CB00007B/2907